Bound for Justice

AGAINST THE ODDS

TORI CARSON

Against the Odds
ISBN # 978-1-78430-971-8
©Copyright Tori Carson 2016
Cover Art by Posh Gosh ©Copyright January 2016
Interior text design by Claire Siemaszkiewicz
Totally Bound Publishing

Published in 2016 by Totally Bound Publishing, Newland House, The Point, Weaver Road, Lincoln, LN6 3QN, United Kingdom.

AGAINST THE ODDS

Dedication

This book would never have been finished without the support of my wonderful husband. I was blessed beyond measure when you entered my life.

I'd also like to dedicate this book to my awesome Facebook reader group, Desired Discipline. Thank you so much for your friendship and kind words of encouragement. Your continued support and help in promoting the books is greatly appreciated.

Chapter One

Fear pervaded every cell of her body. Alexa's throat closed, refusing the smoke laden air. Flames raced through the studio, devouring her dreams. Bolt after bolt of custom woven fabric, designed for her new clothing line, gone in the blink of an eye. Her head throbbed from the beating she'd endured at the hands of her protector and guardian. She pushed away the pain and betrayal. Nothing mattered now but survival. Sliding in and out of consciousness, she lay still, biding her time until she could escape.

One last kick to her ribs, and a muttered obscenity, signaled his departure. Her attacker had ripped her files from the cabinet and scattered them along the floor. Her once priceless, 'one of a kind', designs were now ruined. He'd taken a sledgehammer to her computer's hard drive, wrapped it in a bolt of embellished silk and set it ablaze.

She had to get out and that meant curling into a ball and crying her eyes out would have to wait. As she crawled over months of work, once coveted and protected, now discarded to fuel her funeral pyre, her hand slipped on the loose papers, sending her chin scraping across the blood-soaked floor. She dashed away the tears and continued. As she neared the doorway, she had to move Ezzy's lifeless body from the exit.

Alexa took Ezzy by the arm and pulled her farther into the room. Knowing that Ezzy was beyond help didn't ease the guilt beating at Alexa. Her stomach protested over and over. Bile burned her smoke-scorched throat, her muscles twisted into knots as she fought to keep moving.

Alexa jerked awake, landing hard on the floor beside the single bed in her low-rent apartment. Thousands of miles and ten years later, the bad dreams continued to assault her. The roar of the fire still assaulted her ears. Her lungs still protested the acidic fumes and her stomach still rebelled remembering Ezzy's mutilated body. Long ago, she'd accepted nightmares were a part of her life. She didn't have the time or energy to feel sorry for herself. Betrayal and death were always there waiting for a careless moment. She'd vowed to never be careless again.

* * * *

Sid stared at the young girl's picture taped to his computer screen. It was a tactic he'd used many times while working on cold cases for the FBI. Yet this time was different. He didn't need the photo front and center to keep Alexa on his mind. She lived there. Awake or asleep, it didn't matter, her image was burned into his brain.

He had stacks of other cases littering his workspace and thousands of others just a keystroke away. Why this one?

"Hello," Teague waved his hand in front of Sid's face, "where'd you go?"

"Sorry."

Teague walked over and pulled her photo from the screen. "Missing?"

Sid took the picture and put it back where it had been. His finger lingered over her face. Such a contagious smile and intelligent eyes didn't fit the horrific crimes she was wanted for.

"It's a cold case a buddy of mine in New York asked me to review. Don't worry about it." His friend had long since consigned it to the hopeless case bin, but Sid continued to track down every lead. For whatever reason, he just couldn't shake it. He hated to think about the man hours he'd put into finding the girl. All he really had to go by was a fingerprint.

"Pretty little thing. How long ago did she disappear?" Teague was like a Gila monster, once he sank his teeth into something, he never let go.

"Ten years." She could easily be dead by now. A sixteen-year-old kid wanted by police and living on the streets didn't have a hell of a lot of opportunities.

"Damn. That's a long time. Who do you think grabbed her and why is the NBIA pursing this case?"

The National Border Interdiction Agency, his current employer, specialized in crimes originating outside the United States. "This one is off the clock. She's not a victim. She's an arsonist and a murderer, or so the theory goes." How could a child like that brutally beat and ultimately murder her brother's fiancée, set fire to her family's garment warehouse then stage the scene in an attempt to fake her own death?

"Any leads?" Teague continued to pursue the matter.

Recently he'd been notified of a new hit on the partial print. Unlike the hundreds before it, this one was practically in his own backyard. It seemed doubtful that a young girl would leave the glitz and glamour of New York City to travel across the country and settle in Arizona, but there were some oddities that had his curiosity aroused.

"Maybe."

Teague motioned for him to keep talking.

"Why the hell are you so interested?" Sid wasn't comfortable talking about this case.

"You've been telling me how I need to learn investigative techniques that go beyond a keyboard. Obviously this is something you feel strongly about. You aren't even getting paid for this, yet you're still spending your off time on it. Therefore, it must be a doozy. So walk me through how to solve a ten-year-old case."

Fuck. Why had he believed befriending Teague was a good idea? Although he tried, he couldn't think of a single reason why he shouldn't confide in Teague.

"Recently a local interior design firm was broken into. A secretary, a temp on a six-month assignment, phoned it in. A couple of things caused the investigating officer to be suspicious." He raised his index finger. "First, the temp was supposed to be filling in for a woman on maternity leave. After some digging, he found out there were five secretaries before this one and each had been hired as a six-month temp. And none of them left because they were pregnant." He raised two fingers. "In fact, everyone associated with the firm is hired temporarily or as a contracted project-based employee."

"Could just be cheap. If you keep rotating the staff none of them are going to ask for a raise or expect benefits," Teague suggested.

Sid shrugged. "The owner, a young woman known publically as Sasha, is a big deal. Her designs are the latest craze. Everyone who's anyone has at least a room decorated by Sasha. She isn't hurting for money."

Teague looked at him closely. Sid obviously needed to work on his poker face.

"You and I both know that some of the richest people are the ones that pinch a penny until it screams."

Sid nodded. "According to the police report, once Sasha arrived, she told the investigator there'd been a misunderstanding. She said her boyfriend, who she refused to identify, had ransacked the office after an argument. She told him she was sure nothing had been taken and was adamant he drop the investigation. The detective didn't buy it for a minute and ran the prints anyway."

"Does this Sasha physically match her?" Teague tipped his chin toward the picture.

"The owner of Sasha's Design is a twenty-six-year-old brunette, about five foot six, who reportedly netted several million last year."

"And?"

"So why does she live in a studio apartment in a shitty part of town? According to the DMV, her company owns one delivery van and she personally owns a late-model pickup. Though they are both unencumbered, neither speak of that kind of money. You'd think a young girl earning seven figures would have a few creature comforts."

Teague nodded. "I'm assuming you've had an age progression artist give you a hand."

Sid hit a few keys on his computer and brought up the sketch. About a year ago, he'd asked for a workup. Sid believed in crossing his t's and dotting his i's. His nature dictated he cover every base, though he was sure he wouldn't need it. This case was never far from his mind. Lately, he'd even been dreaming about her. Not the vibrant teen from the picture, but a very serious young woman. A damsel in distress. The type he always fell for.

* * * *

With the reins held loosely between her index and middle fingers, Sasha rode along a faint game trail deep in the Tonto National Forest. The narrow path was barely visible as the sun broke over the horizon, but she knew it well. The breeze, crisp in the morning hours, usually helped dispel the sooty stains destroying her soul bit by bit. Today she found no such reprieve. The smoke cloud, dense and dark, refused to move along. It had taken up residence like a noose swinging above her head.

"What am I going to do, Dakota?" She leaned forward and patted her palomino's neck. He'd been her only true confidant since moving to Arizona. Like her, he'd been abused by the person charged with caring for him. They had so much in common. The steed had grown strong under her ownership, but his emotional distress was still evident. Physically, Sasha had overcome the past. Yet, the haunting nightmares were a reminder that she could run, but never fully escape.

"They found me again," she mumbled into the wind, wishing it weren't true. "I was foolish, Dakota. I'd drawn some sketches one night and left them in the office. They're missing." She sighed. "I'm going to have to run again."

* * * *

Sid tried not to think about the numerous policy violations he was committing as he spent his day off on stake-out in a telephone repair van in the alley behind Sasha's Designs. He was a by the book man. Rules were written for a reason and he believed in following them.

And yet from the first glimpse he'd captured of Sasha Powell, interior decorator extraordinaire, he'd forgotten all about the rules. His muscles, cramped from hours of sitting in seats as ergonomically perfect as the rack, were also pushed from his mind. There was no doubt in Sid's mind Sasha was Alexa Desman, heir to the renowned fashion dynasty, Desman's Designs.

Knowing he'd found her, he brought his laptop online and applied for leave. He couldn't, in good conscience, use agency time for a case not in their jurisdiction, and he wasn't about to let her slip away by investigating half-assed.

For several days Sid tracked her movements. Up before dawn, changing vehicles every day, he learned her routine and determined the best way to approach her. She had money readily available to disappear at a moment's notice. So, showing up with badge in hand was out. He couldn't pull off hiring her as an interior decorator either. His puny little apartment wouldn't warrant someone of her caliber. She could easily assign his business to one of her contract workers.

One morning, he found his opening. Through his extensive research, he'd learned that even as a youth Alexa had been an animal rights activist. She had spearheaded a community fundraiser to help animals suffering smoke inhalation after the 9/11 terrorist attacks. Sasha wasn't a member of any national organizations. However, she was heavily involved with a local horse rescue.

Sid swallowed his pride and called a friend for help. Sammy, a fellow agent who also owned a small ranch near Cordes Junction, answered on the second ring. "I need to ask a favor. How quickly can you teach me to ride?"

He pulled the phone away from his ear as Sammy belly laughed loud enough to bust his eardrums.

"You do realize horses are ridden outside in the" — Sammy gasped dramatically — "dirt. Right?"

"Very funny. Are you going to teach me or not?" Sid wasn't in the mood for a good-natured ribbing.

"Come on out, but I don't want to hear about your laundry bill."

* * * *

Turning into the wind, Sasha hoped to dry her tears before they streaked down her face. *What is there to cry about anyway?* Her life was what she made it. She answered to no one. She tried not to think about the flip side of that, no one to talk to or share her life with. And other than a handful of employees who would miss their next paycheck, no one would mourn if she gave up the fight and fell over dead.

Dakota whinnied as if reading her thoughts. She patted his neck. "I know, boy, I'm going to miss you too. You've been my only true friend. I promise I'll find someone to take good care of you."

Whinnying again, Dakota sidestepped and reared as Sasha struggled to stay in her saddle. Before she could get him under control, a rider crested the bluff and galloped toward her, further spooking the once beaten and abused animal.

From the corner of her eye, she watched him draw a large caliber pistol from the small of his back. Since she'd been a teenager, she'd known her death would be a violent one. Her only regret was not properly ensuring care for Dakota after she was gone.

She heard the shot, but didn't wait for the darkness to claim her. With a flick of the reins, she craned Dakota back in the direction they'd just come and allowed him to bolt. Sasha wasn't prepared for his shoulder to drop halfway through the turn. Her balance shifted and the ground came up to meet her. The rider was on her before she could get to her feet.

The first thing she noticed was fresh blisters on the inside of his index and middle fingers. Her offbeat sense of humor always chose odd times to strike. She could just see herself giving the police a description of her attacker.

'Did he have any distinguishing marks or features?'

'Yes, officer, he had blisters between his fingers.'

The world finally went black and spared her his imagined retort.

* * * *

Desi watched as the latest private investigator he'd hired sauntered through the warehouse toward his office.

"I'll take that finder's fee in cash, Desman." Ritchie wiped the sweat off his upper lip.

Does the asshole really think I earned my reputation by taking shit from weasels like him?

"You should know by now, I don't reward big talk with cash. Show me what you've got or get the hell out of my office." Desman leaned back in his chair, waiting to see what evidence the fat fuck had turned up.

Ritchie ran a finger between his collar and throat before laying a report on Desman's desk. He was perspiring profusely. The smell of onions and garlic permeated the air between them.

Desman's right eye twitched as he read the report. There was just enough information to make Desman sure Ritchie had done the impossible and tracked the bitch down.

"Don't fuck with me. Where's she at? How did you find her?" He didn't bother to hide his fury.

"As soon as I have the finder's fee, you'll have everything you need."

Who the hell does he think he is?

Desman opened his desk drawer. To the left lay the key to the safe, but Desi kept his hand along the right side. He wrapped his fingers around the pachmayr grip of his Glock 10mm and pulled the trigger.

Ritchie's mouth hung open, first probably in shock, then in screaming pain as the bullet and wooden shards from the front panel of Desman's desk embedded deep in his kneecap.

Desman slid back his chair and walked over to where Ritchie was writhing on the floor. He towered above Ritchie. "Bluffing doesn't work with a man holding all the cards," Desi explained, calmly. "Now, being a reasonable man, I'm going to give you two choices. You can give me all the information you have on this girl and live with a bum leg or you can die right now. Choose," he ordered.

Ritchie stared up at him in disbelief. Desman felt a surge of power rush through him.

Tipping his head to one side, Desman warned Ritchie, "Last chance."

"Okay, okay," he gasped between moans. "I'll give you everything I have."

* * * *

From down a long, dark tunnel, Sasha heard a woman whimpering and a man shouting. Her head pounded and she knew she was being a horrible person, but she really wished the girl would just shut the hell up. She should get help for the poor woman. No one could be all right and sound so pitiful, but she couldn't force herself to move.

Slowly, her vision cleared. The yelling man knelt beside her, running his hands all over her body. She wanted to protest, to strike out at his audacity. Why couldn't she move? A deep breath later she realized with shock she was the moaning, injured woman.

"Are you all right?" he asked again.

"You shot me!" Her voice was a mere whisper yet indignation rang clear. Her eyes locked with his, vowing payback.

"I shot the snake," he corrected.

His short, golden brown hair glistened in the sun, giving him an angelic appearance. A pistol packing angel. *Great, now even God wants me dead.* "Snake?" she asked, confused. She hadn't seen a snake.

"Your horse reared as it struck," he continued to explain.

She had to get up. Get away. This man had tried to kill her. Hadn't he? Could there have been a snake? Had she been so out of it she'd missed it? Possibly. Probably. She had to check the trail. If he was telling the truth, the snake would still be there. Using two fingers, she let out a whistle, calling Dakota back to her.

It was difficult to draw air into her lungs. She would be black and blue by morning, but at the moment she didn't feel it. Instead her body thrummed where this stranger with the blistered hands and stunning eyes had touched her. And he'd touched her everywhere.

"Was he bitten? Is he okay?" She struggled to get up.

The man grabbed her forearm and held her still. "Stay calm while I call nine-one-one. Your wrist is broken and you may have other injuries."

"No!" She tried to scramble away, but his grip was deceptively strong. "I'm fine. I just had the wind knocked out of me." She waited for his hold to loosen, drawing her legs underneath her.

When he made no move to let go, she brought her wrist into view. He was telling the truth there. It was definitely broken. Immediately the pain hit, causing her stomach to roll dangerously.

"You need to go to the hospital. You may have internal injuries."

His rich, deep voice soothed her nerves. She had the strangest desire to crawl into his arms and cry a river. Where that came from she didn't know, but it scared her more than being shot at.

Dakota nudged the back of her head. With her free arm she reached around and patted his neck. The moment the stranger let go of her arm, to push Dakota away from her, she used her legs to scoot back and stand up. The wave of pain her sudden movement caused nearly sent her crashing back into the dirt. Through sheer force of will, she stayed on her feet.

Cradling her arm close to her chest, she checked Dakota for wounds. Many people never thought about the animal when a fall took place. Oftentimes, they were hurt far worse than the human. They'd been lucky this time. He was uninjured.

She immediately scanned the trail, looking for evidence of a snake. She wanted to believe him, and for that reason alone she needed him to be a liar. Emotion overwhelmed her when she saw the bloody remains of a rattlesnake just a few feet away.

Why couldn't he have been lying about the snake? It would have made things so much easier.

"Look, my name's Jacob. My truck is just over the rise. I've got a double trailer. Let me drive you into town and we'll get you checked out."

She shook her head. What bad timing!

"Thank you, but no. I'll be fine, really." With her good hand, she caught the reins and climbed into the saddle. It was second nature to seat her boot into the stirrup and swing her leg over his back. She wasn't prepared though, for stars to block out the sun as the world spun precariously. One deep breath told her she'd most likely cracked a rib or two as well. Double damn. She stayed very still until her head cleared. "I've fallen before. I can handle this," she assured him once she was sure she could speak again.

She'd survived much worse, not that anyone would ever know about it. That was one of many secrets she planned to take to the grave.

"I feel responsible. At the very least, let me help you store your gear. If you'd feel more comfortable, I could drive your rig for you. Once we get you to a hospital, I'll call a buddy and have him bring me back out here."

"No, really, I couldn't put you out like that. I'm fine. And thank you for saving my horse." She couldn't bring herself to thank him for taking a life, even if it was a snake. Violence turned her stomach. It always had.

* * * *

Letting her leave was much harder than he'd expected. After following her for days, he knew right where her truck was parked. He waited long enough for her to get back to her rig before he set out after her. He tied Sammy's horse to a mesquite tree a few hundred yards away. Careful to stay near the ground and virtually out of sight behind the rise, he crept between the scrubby bushes and the cholla cactus as he inched closer.

From his vantage point, he could see her clearly. Her struggles to store the saddle caused a physical pain in his chest. Before he could examine the why of it, he was out in the open striding toward her. How many mistakes would he make this morning? How many was one too many?

"Give me that," he commanded, refusing to be pushed aside. Physically taking the saddle from her, he carefully stored it in the open compartment, ignoring her protests and obvious reluctance to have him anywhere near her equipment. It took only a few moments to lead Dakota into the trailer and prepare the rig for departure.

"Wait here while I secure my horse. You're not in any shape to drive yourself out of here." A slew of other comments were stifled before they actually left his mouth. Apparently the agency's sensitivity training had taught him something.

He hadn't reached the mesquite before he heard the diesel motor fire up and take off down the dirt road. Sid cursed up a dust storm. He hadn't been with the woman a total of ten minutes and she had him making deadly mistakes. What was he thinking turning his back on a murder suspect?

Chapter Two

Looking in the mirror, Sasha could almost ignore the bulky white reminder of her carelessness. The cascade of shimmering fabric from her handmade gown concealed most of her cast. She blinked twice, then again, to keep the sudden burning tears captive for a while longer. Sometimes it was hard to think logically and be proud of what she'd accomplished in her life. Her fashions should have been seen on runways in Paris, London and New York. Emotion was an insidious enemy, always attacking when she was least prepared to deal with it.

A small shift of her hips swirled the custom, one of a kind dress, sparking a small glimmer of pride. It was snug across the chest thanks to the wrap holding her cracked ribs in place, but not terribly noticeable. All her bruises were covered, except for the new beauty she'd given herself rolling her hair. The cast on her wrist was proving more harmful than leaving it unbound.

If tonight didn't mean so much to the horse rescue, she'd ditch the dress, slide into her favorite jeans, saddle Dakota and chase the stars across the night sky.

It was time to disappear again. She'd already stayed longer than was safe. And she wasn't sure why. Of course she was tired of running. Tired of starting over. Mostly, she was tired of being alone. She couldn't even take credit for her interior designs. Sasha was just the latest fictional persona in what was growing to be a long list.

Sasha dug her teeth into her bottom lip, refusing to wallow any deeper in self-pity. The money raised tonight would keep the shelter functional for a good six months. That was real and worthwhile.

With her carefully practiced faux smile firmly in place, she pushed open the bathroom door, determined to cajole as much money from these people as she could.

Sid waited in an alcove near the ladies' restroom and bided his time until Sasha appeared. He walked passed her as casually as possible. "I'm looking for the banquet hall. Can you point me in the right direction?"

Recognition flashed across her face. By reflex, it seemed, she touched her wrist at the break. She looked him over carefully, even noting the ugly blisters on his hands. He wished she hadn't noticed. It bothered him to have his appearance be less than perfect.

Sid tilted his head and plastered what he hoped was a shocked expression on his face. "How are you feeling?" he asked, quietly. "I'm glad you sought medical care. I was afraid you wouldn't when you took off." Sid slipped easily into his undercover persona, Jacob.

"I'm fine. Thank you for your concern. I'm heading to the banquet hall, if you'd like to follow me. Dinner should be served any minute." She slipped her injured arm behind her back as if she were ashamed of it. Her other hand touched briefly at her neck before sliding calmly to her side.

Sid was pretty good at reading people. His job depended on it. He'd bet a full week's pay that he'd scared her. *You afraid of all men, or just me?* He stepped back and to the side, offering her his left arm, making it easier for her with the cast.

"I didn't know you were affiliated with the rescue," Jacob ventured, glad to hear his voice remained steady. As her dainty fingers curled around his biceps, his body responded alarmingly. Her touch sent his heart rate spiking and he was suddenly glad his slacks fit a little sloppy. Otherwise everyone in the convention hall would realize he was sporting a hard-on.

"As a business owner, I try to work with a variety of charities." Her voice was cool and detached, signaling this event was nothing more to her than a way to attract perspective clients.

He knew better. Her company did give to various charities, mostly women's shelters and animal rescues. However, this rescue struck a chord. It was the only public event she consistently attended, though no photos containing her likeness were ever publically released. One more reason he was convinced 'Sasha' was in fact Alexa Desman, wanted murderess.

As they entered the hall, Sasha stepped away from him. "Enjoy your dinner." Her cold tone brokered no further discussion. She stepped away from him so quickly he got the impression she didn't want to be seen in public on his arm. He wondered who in the banquet hall had her so concerned. Did she have a romantic interest like she'd told the police? Nothing that he had uncovered pointed in that direction. Could his theory be wrong?

He allowed her to escape him for the time being. He couldn't appear overly interested. If he pushed too hard, and his theory was right, she would run again.

Watching the sway of her hips as she walked away from him caused a stirring he wasn't comfortable with. She was a suspect. A possible murderess. He couldn't risk the case by becoming sexually involved, no matter how exquisite she was.

Sasha had found a place toward the back of the hall that allowed her to keep all entrances and exits within view. She carried herself with the same weary attentiveness as a long-time undercover officer who was used to covering her back and standing alone in life and death situations.

Sid used the decorative mirrors stationed along the walls to keep an eye on Sasha without seeming to. He had barely found his seat before a man approached her. He was in his early thirties, six foot or so and well built. When the man turned slightly, Sid recognized him. He was a popular defense attorney known for representing sports heroes who drove too fast, drank too much or had too short a fuse. Sid was too far away to hear the conversation, but Sasha was on guard. Her stance was a fighter's pose. Feet apart, muscles loose, eyes watching not only the man she was speaking with, but everyone around her too. Her smile rarely faltered, yet she had an aloof quality that kept her apart from everyone else.

After a few minutes, the attorney moved on. Within thirty or forty seconds, another man approached Sasha. This time it was a local news anchor with a less than stellar reputation. Sid was tempted to intervene, but couldn't think of a single reason why it would help his case. Instead he sat and watched as a virtual parade of men talked with Sasha. Every male in the place seemed to want a piece of her time. She greeted each one with a beaming smile that Sid was growing to hate.

He had noticed a few things though. On average, Sasha shook her head 'no' three times with each man. She had also avoided tasting any drinks the men offered her.

In desperation, Sid had changed places at the table. He squinted and watched closely, attempting to read her lips. He was pretty sure she'd said, "Not tonight, I have plans," to several different men.

Once the auction started, he split his attention between the stage and Sasha. To make his appearance seem less contrived, he knew he needed to bid on several items. The first that caught his eye was a sculpture donated by Sasha's Designs. It was modernistic and made from ultra-thin sheets of various alloys. It stood approximately two feet tall and a foot wide. The intertwined circular pieces of copper, brass and zinc were stunning. It reminded him of a desert sunset.

Although he'd love to own such a beautiful piece of art, he knew it would go far beyond his budget. The five hundred he'd laid out for the dinner already had him outside his comfort zone. The challenge he faced was how to bid convincingly without actually winning. He enjoyed watching the facial expressions of the other bidders and bailing before he got stuck. The artisans had donated some amazing pieces and Sasha's stood out beyond them all. One thing was certain, she was a very talented artist.

The evening was coming to a close. Only a handful of items remained on the auction block and he hadn't furthered his cause. Their brief encounter outside the restrooms was, so far, their only conversation. As the men continued to gravitate to Sasha's side, tension swirled in his gut. He was finding it harder and harder not to drag her to a secluded spot and spank that flirty, fake smile right off her face.

One of the auction house employees, a perky blonde with double-D qualifications partially blocked his view while stud number five hundred thirty-seven approached Sasha to make yet another plea. Somehow this one managed to corner her, literally. She was sandwiched with his arm beside her head, boxing her in between a marbleized column and the sponge-painted wall. Sid was well acquainted with this fellow. He was a baseball pitcher with two recent DUIs and a rap sheet for domestic abuse.

While Sid took a moment to decide if stepping in would help or hurt his case, Sasha's pleading eyes met his. Without further thought, he went to her aid. "Misasha," his voice intimate and familiar, "it's been a long evening. Are you ready to leave?" He gripped her hand tightly and began leading her away.

"Who the hell are you?" the pitcher asked with a slight slur to his speech.

"Nobody you want to take on, ball boy," Jacob responded in complete confidence.

Thanking God the Cy Young Award-winning pitcher was drunk and his coordination slowed, Sid deflected the punch that would have cost him several teeth had he mustered his famed ballfield strength. Before the altercation could go any further, a couple of his teammates shouldered the pitcher away.

"It seems I'm in your debt again. Thank you," Sasha whispered in a sultry voice.

He waved off her thanks. "Did you have a good evening?"

"My designs brought in thousands of dollars for the charity." She flashed him that fake as hell smile. "I consider it a success."

Sid rubbed his neck, trying to ease the tension pulsing through his system. Three people were dead because of this woman. He couldn't blow it now. "You didn't eat this evening. Would you like to grab a bite?"

"I was here to raise money. It wasn't a social event for me." She was polite, but distant.

"You were hurt and you've gone an entire evening without food." His tone made his statement a definite censure. He hadn't planned it that way. By the odd look on Sasha's face, she hadn't expected it either. "I'll ask again. Would you please have dinner with me?"

Sasha smiled briefly. "You just ate a very expensive meal. Why would you want to go to dinner with a virtual stranger?"

He'd been closely watching her body language all evening long. When others had approached her, she'd been very much on guard, and while she wasn't exactly relaxed, she was much more at ease. "That dinner was less than edible. I am definitely hungry and you've gotta be too." He held out his hand. "I'm Jacob Erkins, fellow horse lover and business owner."

"Well, Mr. Erkins, I would be happy to have dinner with you as long as you allow me to treat. You've saved me from two difficult situations and I'd like to repay your kindness." She looked like she expected him to balk.

"I don't quite see it that way, but I will take your company any way I can get it. Where would you like to go?"

Eventually they settled on a quiet steakhouse not far from the fundraiser. Knowing how skittish Sasha was, he wasn't surprised when she made up an excuse to drive separately.

Sid watched as Sasha went through the employees only door then he sprinted to the garage. He was glad he had taken his personal car instead of an NBIA stake-out vehicle, giving him the maneuverability to avoid traffic and exit the parking garage ahead of Sasha. He wasn't completely convinced she truly intended to meet him. With that in mind, he quickly did a U-turn and backed into a side street opposite the garage exit.

When her truck appeared and turned in the direction of the restaurant, Sid was unreasonably happy. He tried to tell himself he was excited about gaining some headway in the case, but it was BS and he knew it. Maybe he did deserve that bullet rattling around inside his head, or maybe the bullet was touching on a stupid sector and making him do dumb and careless things. *Yeah, that's gotta be it.* He knew better than to allow a little slip of a woman, who just happened to be the leading suspect in a heinous case, get under his skin.

He stood by the entrance and waited for her, afraid that if he approached her in a dimly lit parking lot she'd get spooked. As she walked up, he noticed she had changed into jeans. "Look at you" — he waved a hand in her direction — "it takes a hell of a woman to look as good in jeans as she did in a stunning evening gown."

A beautiful hint of pink dusted her cheeks as she murmured, "Thanks."

Sid held the door for her and another couple then they walked in together.

"Ms. Sasha," the maître d' greeted her, "it's so good to see you again." The gentleman led them to a secluded booth in the back of the building.

Once seated, the waiter arrived quickly and asked if she'd like 'the usual'.

"Yes, thank you, Jon," she replied without glancing at the menu.

Sid scanned the specials of the day and ordered a salmon filet and steamed vegetables. To avoid an awkward silence, he decided to jump in with questions.

"How badly were you hurt?" He'd been watching her all night long. Besides the cast on one arm, he suspected she'd broken at least one rib. She never took a deep breath and the one time he'd seen her laugh, the color had drained from her face and she'd wrapped her good arm around her chest.

"Bumps and bruises, mostly."

Good girl. She knew better than to reveal a weakness to a possible adversary. "Hmm, methinks the lady doth use the art of understatement."

Sasha jumped nearly out of her skin when an employee sat on the seat beside her.

"Still eating late at night?" The man was sadly shaking his head in tsk, tsk fashion. "But you brought a young man with you. This is new," he went on, obviously sizing up Sid. "We're all talking about it. Tell me the juicy details."

Sasha blushed and closed her eyes as if that would make them disappear. His heart went out to her as he fought to keep a grin from breaking across his face.

He offered his hand across the table. "Jacob Erkins, and you are?"

"I am Roberto, friend to Ms. Sasha and the owner of this establishment." Roberto shook hands vigorously. "Now, how did you two meet? She is a serious girl. Do you think serious about Ms. Sasha? She no cook. This you know? Yes? She eat very late at night. She work too much. This you must fix. She need a man to take her in hand. To take care of her."

"Roberto, go away," Sasha whispered and gently applied pressure on his shoulder.

"You need to eat." Roberto raised her good arm. "Look, she is skin and bones! One meal a day is not healthy, even if it is from the best steakhouse in town. Are you going to feed her?"

"Roberto, pleeeease go away."

"Roberto, how well do you know Ms. Sasha? Can you give me any pointers on how to win her over?"

Roberto slammed his hand down on the table sending the drinks jostling in their glasses. "I knew it! Ms. Sasha, she no talk much. She needs someone to take care of her. You can do this? No?"

"If she will let me, I'd like to apply for the job." He winked at Sasha, unable to keep a grin from surfacing.

"That's enough. Roberto, you're needed in the kitchen. Go away before Marta accuses you of flirting again."

Roberto's grin slipped and he scooted out of the booth. "Be good to her," Roberto advised him and slapped him once on the back.

Sasha hung her head and breathed slowly as if she was struggling to get her emotions together, or maybe she was trying to decide what to say to him. "I'm sorry about that. I have no idea what got into him. Obviously I come here too much. It's close to my office and they have good food," she offered as an excuse.

"It takes a special person to make an impression on a virtual stranger. Don't apologize. You did nothing wrong, except eat too few meals, too late in the day." Sid saw what he suspected was the first real smile she'd given all night.

He had no doubt she was on the run, yet the murder rap didn't feel right. Was his dick doing his thinking for him? He had to admit, it was possible.

Jon arrived with their meals. He felt a little light in the loafers when he looked at Sasha's plate of filet mignon with all the fixings. Hell, he couldn't have put away that much food during his days at Quantico. In all honesty, he'd expected her to be a vegetarian. "How's the palomino you were riding? Was he hurt?"

Her eyes brightened and her expression softened considerably. "It's kind of you to ask. Thank you. He's fine."

"Was he a rescue?" He'd definitely found a way to win brownie points, but he realized he had a genuine interest in the animal. That morning in the desert, the horse had hovered over Sasha with a definite protective streak. Sid respected him for it and was glad he'd been uninjured.

Sasha nodded. "Dakota had been an amazing barrel racer, but when the owner didn't win he took it out on the horse. He still bears the scars from the lashes he received over the years."

"That's terrible. Someone should show the owner what a whip feels like." Sid had expected Sasha to agree with him, instead she cringed and sat farther back in the seat, putting a few extra inches of space between them. "How did you rescue him?"

Sasha took a few more bites before answering him. "I was at an auction when Dakota came across the block. A local man, known for buying cheap horses and trucking them across the border to slaughterhouses, was bidding on him. I couldn't stand the thought of that happening to him...any horse really. Tonight's fundraiser will allow the rescue to purchase, and thus save, many more."

"The US outlawed horsemeat consumption for humans." Sammy had been talking his ear off about it a year or so ago. At that time, Sid had never even touched a horse so he hadn't listened very carefully.

"That's true, but it didn't stop them from slaughtering them and shipping the meat overseas or using it in pet food. Just recently we got legislation passed making that illegal. Yet they can still transport the live animals across the border to the slaughterhouses down there."

He liked that she fought her battles through the legal system, but wasn't naïve enough to think it would remove loopholes and other nefarious concerns. "How long have you been championing their cause?"

"I'm no one's champion. The ladies that run the foundation are the heroes. I simply help with fundraising. Tell me about your horse. It takes a lot of training for an animal to remain calm around the noise of a firearm."

He didn't know that. Hell, he hadn't even considered it when he fired his weapon. "I can't take credit for that. He's a retired military horse." This was not a subject he could afford to discuss. "Your art pieces were highly sought after. The rescue must be pleased."

She shrugged. "I saw you bid on a few items. I'm sorry it didn't work out."

"I was there primarily to lend my support. I hadn't expected to walk away with anything." Maybe talking about her artwork would give him a few clues to her past. "Your statues reminded me of Robert Glen's Mustangs. Have you spent any time in Texas?"

Another smile lit her face. "Wow, that's quite the compliment. Thank you. Have you followed his work?"

"A little. I lived in Las Colinas for a bit. His statues were so lifelike I did some research on the man." Sid had found it was best to stay as close to the truth as possible while working undercover.

"As a young girl, I was fascinated by his work."

Sid loved how animated Sasha became when she spoke about a passion of hers. He wondered what else would bring a flush to her cheeks and a shine to her eyes. Her smile had a strange remote control effect on his cock. Every time she granted him a genuine smile, his dick would twitch. It was disconcerting, but not unpleasant. "I suspect you were a very headstrong little girl."

She tipped her head to the side and seemed to be sizing him up. "You were probably a very serious boy. The kind all the teachers loved."

He laughed for the first time in days. "And most of the kids hated. Let me guess, you were one of the popular kids, homecoming queen or prom queen."

Her smile disappeared and she stared at her plate as she shook her head. "Nothing like that." She grabbed her glass and took a long drink from her iced tea.

Because you were on the run? Her sad expression bothered him. "I was always odd man out. Much like tonight. Here I sit in a tux while you're dressed in jeans like everyone else in the restaurant."

"Yes, being better dressed than everyone else is a fate worse than death. It was very selfish of me." She hid her smirk, but amusement was obvious in her voice.

Not only had she turned the tables on him, but she'd successfully avoided answering any questions that would help him fill in the blanks about her history. "I have no complaints. You look pretty damn amazing in those jeans."

"Why thank you. I'm certainly enjoying the view," she admitted as a blush stole across her cheeks.

He caught himself squaring his shoulders and sitting a little taller in the booth. Damn, he was acting more like a man trying to impress his date than a federal agent.

A shadow fell across Sid's face as Jon placed the check on the table. Fuck, it was too soon. He wanted to see where this conversation would lead. Before had the chance to pursue it, Sasha threw several large bills onto the tray and moved to stand up. Sid knew the moment was gone. He handed the bills back to her and watched her eyebrow quirk upward. In a soft, conspiratorial tone, he pleaded, "Please allow me to get this. Roberto wouldn't approve of a lady paying for a gentleman. I rather enjoyed the food and would like to be able to come back."

He was granted another real smile.

"Okay," she conceded. "But I still owe you a meal."

"And I intend to hold you to it." While he paid the bill, Sasha used the restroom. Or at least that was her story. Sid was less than surprised when fifteen minutes later he went outside to find her truck gone.

* * * *

"Sasha," she made it a point to use her assumed name even when talking to herself, "you're such a chicken! Would it have killed you to actually finish a date?" Well, she conceded, it might. If he wasn't what he appeared, walking out of the restaurant alone with him could have been a deadly mistake. That, however, was not the reason she had run.

Those soft blue eyes, full of compassion, were more dangerous than the pistol he'd brandished on their first meeting. When he'd turned his focused gaze on her, she'd felt the jolt all the way to her core.

In the hallway, Sasha had made the mistake of resting her hand on his well-defined biceps. His obvious strength should have been a warning to keep her distance, yet she'd caught herself leaning toward him, wanting to be engulfed by those strong arms and cuddled safely against his wide chest.

Sasha paced the length of her apartment. It was the same thing every night. She didn't bother with lights. It was safer without them. She had learned that the hard way too.

At first she'd been afraid of the dark. She would turn on every light and leave them on until sunrise. One unwanted guest later with a knife practically longer than her arm had taught her lights only showed the predators where you were. They did not keep bad things from happening.

Footsteps outside her door sent her stomach into knots. Every muscle taut, ready to bolt should the sounds not continue on past. A woman's drunken giggle allowed her to breathe again. It was just the guy down the hall bringing home another companion. She recognized his footfalls, heavy steel-toed boots, with a long confident stride.

Sasha knew the sounds of the building. Sometimes it made her crazy, listening to the lives of others. Like a ghost, she was a witness to their goings-on without ever being a part of them. Night after night she paced and listened, growing envious. Even the couple above and to the north, with their constant fighting, had more of a life than she did. And the noises coming from their apartment after the fights had her blushing.

It was easy to slip into a good old-fashioned pity party. She had tried to date a couple of times. It had never turned out well. What had she been thinking, meeting Jacob for dinner? He reminded her of Simon, a wealthy business owner she had contracted with when she'd lived in Denver. It had seemed perfect until he'd sold her out and two men had been waiting for her at his home.

Was Jacob another Simon? It didn't feel right. He could have grabbed her that morning out in the desert. He'd had a gun. No one had been around. If he worked for her enemies, she'd already be dead.

Could he be the one who had broken into her office? It was possible. Maybe he was searching for evidence of her true identity. She'd been sloppy, leaving copies of her clothing designs in her place of business. It was time to leave.

The thought sent a bucketful of despair straight to her heart. She didn't think she could. Not again.

Sasha gave in to the inevitable. Dressed for the night, she snuck out the back of her tiny apartment. There would be no sleeping. She had too much on her mind, too much adrenaline rushing through her system.

She had actually gone on another date—*holy shit!* What had gotten into her? Yes, Jacob had the bluest eyes she'd ever seen and a physique meant to be ogled, but what was that in the big picture? Her body knew the answer. It amounted to an incredible case of sexual frustration! What was the female equivalent to blue balls?

* * * *

Sid slowed as he drove past her apartment complex. In his research he'd learned she paid her lease in full in six-month intervals. That was virtually unheard of in the low-income neighborhood she lived in. He drove around back and parked in the alley a block away. Using night-vision goggles, he was able to see as if it were day. He had no idea what he was doing or what he was looking for. He just knew he couldn't go home.

Within moments of parking his car, he witnessed a small figure climbing out onto the virtually nonexistent window ledge. It was difficult to tell for sure, but it certainly appeared to be Sasha. He was debating exiting his vehicle when he watched in abject horror as the petite figure clad all in dark clothing dove backward from the second story ledge. Without conscious thought he punched nine-one-one into his cell phone and started the engine of his car, intent on speeding to the site of her suicide.

Before he could throw his car into gear, his breath stilled in his lungs as her hand gracefully connected with the fire escape ladder and slid down it to mere feet from the pavement. Bile choked his throat. The hammering of his heart drowned out the operator asking the nature of his emergency. He knew the daredevil acrobat was Sasha. His nearly paralyzing fear quickly turned to anger as he remembered her previous injuries and her lack of personal concern.

"Never mind," he told the operator before sliding from his car. Sid stayed in the shadows and followed her. In the dead of night, she traversed alleyways owned by drug users and gang members. And he would bet a month's salary she did so unarmed. The urge to shake some sense into her was almost too hard to resist. Roberto had been right when he'd said someone needed to take her in hand, and Sid vowed to do just that even if it took handcuffs to accomplish it.

After she crossed Nineteenth Avenue, Sid lost sight of her. His heart was hammering in his chest. Two men stood under the pale yellow streetlight. The man closest to him had a bulge near his ankle, no doubt it was a gun. He stayed in the shadows, watching them exchange a package for cash. Once the men left the corner, Sid crossed the street, hoping to catch a glimpse of her.

Where in the hell is she? Dressed in dark gray, she moved silently, making it nearly impossible to track her movements in the dim lights of the city. For over a mile he had trailed her.

His left hand rubbed the back of his neck. He had more questions than answers. Where was she going? How often had she walked these dangerous streets alone? Why all the secrecy? Most important of all, what could possibly be worth this risking of her life?

A rat skittered out of a side road, Polk Street, if he wasn't mistaken. He stood perfectly still listening to the sounds of cars. It amazed him how much traffic there was even in the wee hours of the morning. Glancing down the avenue, he could see a woman selling her wares on Van Buren. Without any promising leads, he headed down Polk.

Movement caught his eye, a small figure scaling the block fence of a storage lot. The odds were a million to one it was Sasha, but he followed anyway. To Sid's relief, the area was dim and the asphalt gummy from the sun beating on it all day. It allowed him to move quickly in relative silence. He got within a few yards, just close enough to be sure it was indeed Sasha. He watched as she unlocked the padlock on a climate-controlled storage unit. He had no chance to look inside. The door slid open only high enough for her to scoot underneath then was quickly lowered again. Sid took note of the address and unit number, planning to pay it a private visit.

* * * *

Desman looked at the sketches. He'd seen them before. Oh, not these exact sketches, but there was no mistaking the artist. It was time to tango. He picked up the phone and made the call, dialing the number by heart. This time the bitch would not escape him. There could be no further slip-ups. "There's a bolt that needs returned to the fold," he informed his most cut-throat associate. He was perfect for this assignment once set on the trail he never came back empty-handed.

"Right away, Mr. Desman."

He crumpled the sketch and tossed it into the can beside his desk. Once he had his hands on her again, he'd settle a couple of scores. Even Hawkings, the pain in the ass attorney in charge fiscally of both Desman's Designs and his trust fund, would have to admit Alexa had been on the run all this time. He wasn't sure what he was looking forward to most, crushing Hawkings or ending Alexa and finally getting the inheritance that was due him.

Chapter Three

Sasha arrived at work early. She went into her office and locked the door. All night long she had avoided the inevitable. Now it was decision time. Did she stay and fight, or run?

What the hell was there worth staying for? On the other hand, what was the purpose in running? Her existence could scarcely be called a life. Her only friend was an abused horse who needed a real home as badly as she did. Could spending an hour in the company of a man really make her change her entire way of existing?

Apparently, yes. During her dinner with Jacob, she'd felt alive for the first time in years. Naturally she'd had to stay on her toes, censor her responses and remember all her lies, but she had let her guard down a bit and damn, it had felt good. The way he'd looked at her... A shiver went down her spine. Maybe what she needed was to get laid. Women had needs too.

The situation was similar to Simon, yet Jacob was so different. Simon had been all over her, always touching her in some way or asking probing questions. Jacob talked to her, he didn't question her, and other than checking her for injuries that morning in the desert, he'd never touched her.

Was that the appeal? The fact that his gaze alone could set fire to her panties? She kept replaying their time together. Whenever he'd looked at her, she'd felt as if he was seeing the real woman, the woman buried underneath so much baggage no one should even guess at her existence. He made her feel vulnerable, yet protected. What would it be like to have one person on this earth who she could be herself with, to let her hair down and share all her deep dark secrets with and know he would still be there for her? A woman would do anything for a man like that.

"Ms. Powell?"

The disembodied voice of her secretary sent her jumping out of her chair. She'd completely lost track of where she was and that she wasn't alone. Maybe a quickie was what she needed to get her mind off Jacob's wide shoulders and toned ass.

"A Mr. Erkins is here to see you."

Or not! Now faced with the opportunity, she felt much less confident and very embarrassed for her wayward thoughts.

Sasha ignored the intercom and picked up the phone to speak in private. "I really can't be disturbed right now. Please make an appointment with Mr. Erkins for later in the day and give him my apology for any inconvenience this may cause." She hung up before Number Five could argue.

She buried her face in her hands, knowing her behavior was getting her nowhere. Straightening her shoulders and calming her runaway hormones, she picked up the phone and called several textile distributers. After her immediate business needs were taken care of, she grabbed her purse and planned to once again slip away from the handsome Mr. Erkins. She'd let her secretary tell him she'd been called away on urgent business.

"Ms. Powell, I'm so glad I chose to wait."

Sasha stopped in mid step. She felt the blood drain from her face as she swung her head in his direction.

There was no mistaking the deep timbre of his voice. A flush quickly spread through her and a smile teetered on her lips until she noticed his rather large physique perched on the corner of her secretary's desk. Secretary number five, soon to be replaced by six, had her assets showcased. A healthy dose of misplaced jealousy smacked her right upside the head, making it impossible to think her way out of the situation.

While she stood there searching for a new lie to tell, he gently took her by the arm and led her back into her office. His touch sent a sizzle right to her core. She pulled away from him and took her place behind the mammoth desk. She sat as regally as possible and gave him her best 'princess indulging a peasant' look. "What can I do for you, Mr. Erkins?"

He watched her for a few moments and she had to fight the urge to squirm under his direct gaze.

Slowly Jacob crossed his arms and stared down at her solemnly. "So, is it bad breath or body odor that sends you running away from me every chance you get?"

Sasha tipped her head down toward her desk, trying in vain to hide the grin spreading across her face. He just couldn't be another plant looking to take her to jail, or worse, back to her brother. Regaining her composure, she steepled her fingers and looked him straight in the eye. "Both, of course."

The moment of silence ended with both of them cracking up.

"You're a mean woman, Misasha."

She certainly wasn't 'his' as the term 'mi' implied, and she wasn't sure how she felt about him calling her that. Her girly parts were all enamored though, standing at attention and making demands while her mind was sending up warning flags. Unfortunately, fire conquered the ice. Those flags went up in lustful flames as he reached across her desk and took her hand in his.

"I promise, I showered and brushed my teeth just a couple of hours ago, so it should be safe enough to have lunch with me."

"You're a goof!" She could hardly think with his thumb brushing the back of her hand. Had all her nerve endings migrated there in a desperate attempt for attention? "Sure, we can do lunch. Where would you like to go?" Her voice sounded odd. Not at all her own. Panic began to build as she realized she'd agreed to another date.

"Does Roberto serve lunch? I might need his advice. He seems to have a way with women. Perhaps I could learn a few things from him."

Her face heated and she wished she could hide. "I may never go back there again." Why did he have to be funny? This would be easier if he were arrogant or hard on the eyes. "How about the salad bar across the street?"

"No way," he answered, shaking his head. "Man does not live on rabbit food and it would be too easy for you to slip away from me again. My ego can't take too many more events like that."

"I think your ego is holding up just fine." She rose from her desk and walked out of her office with him. "How about that new sandwich place on Central Avenue?"

"There's a bunch of those springing up. Good idea, let's give it a try. I'm parked over here." He pointed to his late-model BMW.

"I have some errands to run afterward. I'll meet you there."

He stopped in place and sniffed his arm. "Nope, nothing there." Holding his hand in front of his mouth, he audibly exhaled. "Nope, nothing offensive there either." He clutched his heart dramatically. "You're killing me here, Misasha. Cut me some slack. I promise to do the speed limit, stick to public roadways, refrain from texting or using my cell phone, whatever it takes."

"Jacob..." She cringed at her conciliatory tone. She needed to be in charge. "I don't want you to get the wrong impression. I'm a busy woman with a business to run. I don't usually take lunch at all. You've been very kind to me, helped me out of two difficult situations and you seem like a nice man, but I'm not looking for a relationship right now." *And if I spend much more time with you, I'm going to do something really stupid.*

"Good, neither am I. I'm looking for a lunch date and I have it on very good authority that you need to eat more. I'm trying to be a Good Samaritan. Now, let's help save the planet and reduce our carbon footprint by only taking one car."

She couldn't help but smile. "Does that line actually work for you?"

"I don't know. I've never tried it before. What do you think would work better? I'm batting a zero here."

"Do you promise to ask for directions if we get lost?" Teasing him felt intimate, as if she'd made a connection with him. She didn't feel so utterly alone in the world.

"And give up my man card? Lady, you drive a hard bargain." He made a point of shifting his weight and shaking his head. "Okay, if we get lost I promise to ask for directions. Now will you allow me to drive you to lunch?"

She was crazy to get into a car with a man she barely knew. Obviously someone was on to her, otherwise the break-in made no sense. He could easily kill her and dispose of the body without anyone knowing or caring. And yet, she nodded and allowed him to lead the way. *What an idiot!*

She felt better as the driveway neared and nearly sick as they drove right past it. Remaining as calm as her churning stomach would allow, she pointed to the restaurant they'd agreed to. "Um, Jacob, I think you really do need to stop for directions. We just passed it." Her heart beat double time remembering another date gone awry.

"I don't like that one. I'm going to the one off Bethany."

She tried to take a calming breath. Okay, it wasn't reasonable, but it might be truthful. "Why?" she asked, reserving judgment. Sasha gripped the door handle, ready to make a quick getaway if need be. She was ashamed that she wanted him to have a plausible excuse. It had nothing to do with her safety. She genuinely liked Jacob.

"For the same reason I didn't like the salad bar. It's too close to your office. You'll find some excuse and slip away from me." He reached over and took her hand.

Without even thinking about it, she linked her fingers with his. She looked out of the window, shielding her expression. His touch was addicting and she was desperate for more. "I'm never going to live that down, am I?"

"Not likely," he teased.

Again, his smile sent a jolt of cosmic-powered lust straight through her. She didn't understand that either. She'd never had a truly pleasurable sexual experience. Why would she think it would be any different with Jacob? She sure had more chemistry with him than any other man. Was it instant attraction or did her need for human companionship have her sitting next to a paid assassin?

True to his word, they arrived safely at the agreed upon restaurant, just not the location she'd had in mind.

Sasha figured the best defense was a good offense. After giving their orders, she decided to jump right in. "So, Jacob, at the gala you said you owned your own business."

He nodded. "I do computer systems analysis."

Sasha wrinkled her nose like he had a disease. "I never would have pegged you for a computer geek."

"Thank you. I think. How did you get started with interior decorating?"

She had many pat answers, yet for some reason none of them came to mind. So much of her life was a farce that she felt more like an actress on a stage than a real person. What harm was there in giving a small glimpse of the real her? "I think geometrically. Shapes, colors, textures just form patterns in my brain. Apparently that's different than most people." Turning on her high wattage smile, she emotionally stepped back a bit, feeling as if revealing even that small piece of herself had been too much. She tipped her head downward, allowing her hair to partially shield her face. "Or so I believe. Having only had access to this one brain—I could be wrong."

"Then I'll be kind and never invite you to my apartment. The chaos of it all might overload your sensory receptors." Jacob reached out and brushed her bangs away from her eyes.

She leaned her head into his touch. "A challenge! I love it." He'd looked at home in both jeans and formal wear. At the gala she'd watched him often, yet she'd never caught him fussing with his attire. She wondered what his home really looked like. "I also think you underestimate your style." She smiled again, amazed that she was enjoying herself. Bantering with him gave her a giddy feeling. "Unless someone dresses you each day."

"Are you applying for the job?" His voice was low and speculative.

"Could be. I'm in a ruffles and bows phase right now. Do you think that would work for you?" She shook, trying to keep her giggles silent.

"You are definitely a mean woman, Misasha." He shook his head. "The ruffles are out." He paused as a devilish expression crossed his face. "But the bows I may be able to work with. Bows remind me of presents. Presents are unwrapped and are then a source of pleasure. So if you promise to unwrap me each evening, I might be persuaded to wear a bow — somewhere inconspicuous."

She felt her face redden. "I suppose I deserved that one," she admitted. The thought of seeing him naked sent her blood pressure spiking in her erogenous zones. Changing the subject seemed like a great idea, and work was the only thing that quickly came to mind. "What exactly does a computer systems analyst do?"

"I design software for both corporate and government applications," he answered simply then took a bite of his sandwich.

"Are we talking accounting spreadsheets or firewall protection?" Her heart started to beat a little faster.

Learning about computer systems might help her get the edge over her brother.

"If it involves a hard drive, I can write a program for it. Are you looking for something specific for your company?" He sounded truly curious.

"I know very little about technology. I'm more of a paper and pencil girl." She twisted her earring nervously. If he helped her learn about computers it would mean a great deal of alone time with Jacob. Sasha was finding it hard to remember why that might be a bad thing.

"You have a website. I checked it out after the gala."

"You checked me out? How forward of you!" Her eyes widened in mock irritation. For the first time in longer than she could remember, she tried using a flirty voice.

Jacob chuckled. "I'd be willing to offer you my services." He flashed her an endearing smile where only the right side of his mouth quirked upward, as if he were trying to remain serious, but just couldn't.

"What sort of services do you think I need, Jacob?" Her voice was purposefully soft and sexy. She knew better than to be so forward.

"I'd be willing to protect your hard drive from unwanted penetration." He winked at her.

"Mr. Erkins, do you really believe my hard drive is easily penetrated?" she enquired with a feigned haughty tone she'd perfected years ago.

Jacob's eyebrows rose and a slightly amused expression danced across his handsome face. "Not likely, Ms. Powell. Not likely, but I'm willing to offer my protection, just in case."

"Before you could properly protect my 'assets', wouldn't I have to give you access to them?" Bantering with him was fun and it gave her a naughty thrill.

Pathetic, really. Yet on a different level entirely, the wheels were turning. Could Jacob be the key to ending this nightmare once and for all? If he taught her how computers were compromised, then maybe she could get some hard evidence on her brother.

"I promise to be discreet and keep your best interests as my first priority."

His voice caressed her senses and caused dangerous stirrings. When had she become such a flirt? Every time she tried to trust someone it ended in disaster. Was she a hopeless romantic or a fool? "What about download speeds? I've been told I'm a bit slow in that department."

"One thing our businesses have in common is a need to see to every detail. Perhaps the problem isn't with your speed, it's with other people's perception of your needs."

"And you know about my needs?" She seemed hyper tuned to his every move. Each time his lips parted to take a bite, she imagined them sliding down her neck, surrounding her nipple. Pulling it deeply into his mouth. She quickly took a drink of a water. Something, anything, to break the spell. This was turning dangerous. His striking blue eyes held her captive. Her erogenous zones were sending up flares, demanding attention. She needed some relief and soon. Did she dare?

"If given the opportunity, I would be intimately aware of your needs and take great pleasure in seeing to each and every one." He slid a finger down her cheek.

Her heart skipped a beat. Time to back up and take a reality check, otherwise she was going to jump over the table and start ripping off his clothes. Sitting up straighter, she forced her brain to function. "To become an expert in penetration protection, I imagine you must have in-depth experience in smooth-talking your way around a girl's firewalls."

He sat farther back in the booth, as if he'd sensed the change in her. "I admit I've had extensive experience hacking into computers. If you're asking me about other experiences I've had, I'd have difficulty answering that. After spending an afternoon in your company, I'm having trouble remembering anything before our misadventure in the desert."

Run, Sasha, run! This guy is way too dangerous. Obviously, he was lying. And yet, everything about him seemed sincere. Her hormones had to be overloading her common sense. Maybe a quickie was what she needed. With the right guy could sex really be like those romance novels she read so often? Or was it one more piece of fiction like the families portrayed in sitcoms? As much as she wished life was warm and fuzzy, she knew it wasn't.

"You are clearly out of my league, Mr. Erkins."

His head cocked slightly to one side, an emotion flittered darkly across his handsome features.

"I'm not sure how to take that." His voice took on a slight edge. "The night of the gala you had quite an entourage."

She nodded, remembering the various men who'd approached her that evening. "Those events are always the same. Men with too much power and money to bother being civil. Their reasons for attending the event were less than altruistic. For most, it was a publicity stunt or a networking opportunity, but their money could mean the difference between life and death for the animals at the rescue."

Jacob, on the other hand, had rarely left his seat. He'd bid on items that she could see him using rather than those sure to give him a write-up in the newspaper. She could be wrong, but he'd seemed to be there for the betterment of the animals. He didn't win any of the auctions, but she'd seen him put an envelope in the donation box.

He was gazing at her as if she'd insulted him.

"So, yes, when I was approached I did smile and make small talk with men who thought I'd look good on their arm during a publicity photo and perhaps sprawled across their bed for an evening of fun. But I wasn't foolish enough to encourage their advances."

The coffee Jacob was drinking damn near spewed across the table.

"I'm sorry." Her face instantly turned red. "That was in amazingly bad taste. I'm a little jaded by their would-be attention. And some of them, as you noticed, just don't take no for an answer."

"What have I done that makes you think I belong in that same category?" He tried to keep his voice neutral, as if the question was only a matter of curiosity.

Her eyes widened as she reached across and touched his hand. "Oh no, Jacob, that's not what I meant. Not at all. You're nothing like them. Among other things, I believe you'd take no for an answer."

"Ball boy did seem persistent," he agreed. Sid ran the memory back in his mind. That evening her facial expressions had been rather plastered on, not in the least sincere. Her high wattage smile had attracted a number of men, but it hadn't reached her eyes. Though he heard it rarely, her laugh, which was potent enough to turn his spine to Jell-O, was nothing like the polite chuckle she'd used during the gala. And she had eaten dinner afterward with him. Apparently, a pretty face and a large bank account didn't turn her head.

"So, why am I out of your league?" he asked, again refusing to let it drop. Yes, he had an ulterior motive, but it wasn't about getting her in his bedroom. If he told himself that enough, it might become the truth. He hadn't laid a hand on her, yet. He was willing to admit strangling her held a certain appeal. She was the most stubborn woman he'd ever met. Her gymnastic stunt out the window of her apartment scared him as few things had before.

"Jacob, you seem like a very nice man." She was staring at the table as if she couldn't bear to look at him.

While he waited for the 'but', he took stock of his emotions and wasn't pleased with his analysis. This was about a murder case, not a relationship or even getting laid. She was messing with his head, changing his priorities, and that was unacceptable.

Her soft sigh sent another zinger straight to his groin. What the fuck? Why couldn't he focus around her? Actually, he was focused all right, but with his dick not his brain.

"Honest and real," she went on, unaware of the arrows she was shooting through his conscience. "You have no idea how appealing that is. My business is built around lavish façades. Nothing is real."

Sid forced himself to get control and keep his facial expressions blank. She was showing him a glimpse inside her world. He was ashamed of himself. Damn it, he was just doing his job. Three people were dead and this woman, incredible though she may be, was believed to be the murderer.

She sat up straight, touched her right earring and flashed him her fake smile. "I'm just starting my business and I can't afford to have my attention divided. I have my life savings wrapped up in this company and the competition is fierce. At this point in my life, I'm just not in a position to start a relationship."

He calmly nodded while a tiny burst of triumph spread through his gut. He knew she'd lied and now he'd learned one of her tells. In his business, things like that mattered. "I completely understand, Sasha. My company is thriving, but it's still in the early phases. I travel a lot. My frequent flier miles look like the national debt." He laughed, buying time to figure out what he needed from her. He had to keep the lines of communication open and get her guard down. "What I'd like, for now," he conceded, "is a lunch buddy — when we aren't off meeting clients." He leaned forward and in a conspiratorial whisper he added, "Roberto is counting on me. I wouldn't want to let him down."

She laughed like he'd known she would. Some of the shadows left her eyes. This case just didn't make sense. What could she have gained by killing the girl and destroying the factory? From what he could see, nothing. And the brutality with which the girl had been killed really didn't fit with the woman he was beginning to know. So, where did that leave him?

He needed to check out her storage rental. He knew it had been leased at the same time as her apartment. It, too, was paid six months in advance with cash.

"When it works out, I'd love to have lunch with you." Sasha jumped when her cell phone beeped. She gave it a quick glance. "I'm sorry. I have to get back. I have a meeting."

Sid noticed Sasha's knuckles were white as they drove back to her office. Once they pulled up outside her business, she let out a breath. Looking at her closely, he noticed dots of perspiration along her forehead. It appeared that being in a vehicle alone with him pushed her limits to the max. He wondered what the hell kind of life this woman really lived.

Chapter Four

Sid was fairly sure he had until nightfall before Sasha would revisit her storage unit. He'd been tracking her for some time now, yet he wouldn't have known about the place if he hadn't caught the brief glimpse of her slipping out the night before. His heart stuttered remembering her fragile form, complete with cast, flipping over the railing and slinking around a gang-infested neighborhood in the dark of night. Oh, how he'd like to shake some sense into the girl. He had double-checked the tracking device he'd planted on her truck and it confirmed she was never near the storage unit. He had to admit the subterfuge had his curiosity piqued.

With a little luck, he'd soon have some answers to his many questions. All he needed to worry about was tripping a security feature. If she had surveillance video and he didn't circumvent it, this investigation would be over before it began in earnest. After scaling the roof, he checked all the units in her section. Other than the cheesy-ass equipment installed by the building's owner, it looked to be clean.

After he'd been shot, he'd spent months riding a desk in a cyber unit. He was confident he could circumvent most security systems and hack into just about any computer or software program available on the market.

Still, the roll-up door concerned him. He couldn't spot any security beyond the common variety hardware store lock. Considering the elaborate cloak and dagger shit she'd pulled coming here, it didn't make any sense at all.

He checked the door again, this time with an EMF meter. Still no hint of an electrical draw that would come from a security system. Cautiously, he jimmied the lock. Inching the door open just a crack, he checked yet again. This case was too important to make a sloppy mistake. His gut churned. He would have felt better if he'd found something. She was too on edge to only use a common variety key lock.

With his heart in his throat, he lifted the door far enough open to slide underneath. Immediately he noticed a white powder on his clothing that hadn't been there before. An emotion he didn't even recognize started to choke him. Drugs! Could she be mixed up in the drug trade? Damn, he hadn't seen that coming. He lay on the floor, just inside the doorway, scanning the area for evidence of a security system he was fast believing was non-existent and took stock of the situation.

In recent years, Desman's Designs had been tightly linked with one of the East Coast mobs. They were reputed to have a hand in everything from gambling to drugs to human trafficking. Drugs made sense. He should have considered it long before now. This case was never far from his mind. Lately, it haunted his every thought, and yet he'd never considered drugs as a motivator. Why?

Alexa had been just a teenager when the murders occurred. Already a talented designer—the accepted theory for the case evolved around professional jealousy. The brother and co-owner of Desman's Designs had decided to go with another designer for that year's New York debut. In a fit of temper, Alexa had supposedly killed her, destroyed her designs and set fire to the warehouse, killing two seamstresses caught in the blaze.

Nothing linked her in any way to drugs. Logically though, it fit. Still, his gut told him no way. Could he trust his instincts with his dick involved?

While his thoughts rampaged through his brain, he rubbed the white substance between his fingers, knowing better than to taste it. This wasn't some television drama. He had no desire to taste Draino or worse. He brought it to his nose and frowned. It smelled familiar—and comforting. He swore under his breath. He'd found her security system. Son of a bitch! Talc. Her security system was talcum powder on the floor by the door.

Scanning the unit, he frowned. Several dress forms stared accusingly at him. They were clothed in what appeared to be very expensive fabric, but looking closely he saw pins holding pieces together. If there had been any doubt in his mind, it was gone now. He had definitely found Alexa Desman, missing heir and wanted murderess.

He should've rolled back under the door, replaced the lock and notified his superiors. Yet he couldn't bring himself to do it. This case had gotten under his skin. He couldn't turn her over to anyone else, even if it did mean his career was at stake.

The last time he'd violated policy, he'd ended up with a lead souvenir lodged inside him. When would he learn? Apparently not today. Instead he cleaned the talc from both the floor and his clothing while he surveyed the rest of the room. The boxes surprised him. She was getting ready to move again. Had he pushed her too hard or did this link back to the break-in at her office?

The unit was bare save for a few boxes near the entrance and a couple others on a metal shelving unit, a partially sculpted bust, the dress forms, two file cabinets that turned out to be empty and a laptop. The venting system criss-crossed the roof and the lighting flickered and hummed annoyingly. Sid methodically went through the containers scattered near the doorway. Most were filled with clothing design sketches. Near the bottom of the last box, he found a locked metal safe. As he set to open it, a faint sound outside the unit caught his attention, an indistinct scraping noise like something rubbing against the metal door.

Quickly, he grabbed her laptop, scaled the farthest shelf, scooted as far back as possible and waited, hoping the air ducts and boxes obscured him from view.

If Sasha had broken from her routine and arrived while it was still light out, he had a major problem. The lock was still in the metal hasp, but it wasn't latched and she couldn't help but notice the talc had been swept into a pile. If she escaped him now, it would take months or years before he found her again. He muttered expletives under his breath.

Sid remained motionless as the door slid through the track just above his body. From his hiding place, he scrutinized the intruder, noting the pistol at home in his right palm. He looked familiar, but Sid couldn't place him. Seeing an intricate tattoo of a clock with daggers as hands just below the man's ear made the hairs on the back of Sid's neck stand on end. While he couldn't put a name to the man, the tat was a well known East Coast gang affiliation symbol for a made man or a paid killer. This guy was bad news. Careful to keep his weight from shifting, he pulled his cell phone from his pocket and began snapping photos of the man and the tattoo. The angle was bad, but he dared not move.

Sid was disappointed when he noticed the man was wearing gloves, but not surprised. His movements were calm, quick and efficient. The thought of him anywhere near Sasha scared the hell out of him. Could this be the boyfriend Sasha had told the local police about? If so, he would never figure out women and their taste in men.

Knowing he had started a chain of events he had no hope of containing, he clicked a few more pictures, swiped a quick message and sent it to the only person he knew that was better with a computer than he was. Their friendship was only a few years old, but forged in the fires of hell.

Quicker than expected, Teague sent him a text back.

Randall Hackman. Aka the Hatchet. Half the branches of the FBI on the East Coast are looking for this guy. He went off the radar three days ago. He made his first kill at the tender age of thirteen. He's the enforcer of choice for several families. He specializes in 'asset retrieval'. His associates are gobbling up Mr. G's share of the human slave trading market.

No one knew more about Mr. G's business than Teague. He'd spent most of his adult life trying to take the man down. Two years ago, he'd finally succeeded. Unfortunately, it had done little to stem the tide of crime. Others had quickly filled the void. With the advent of the internet, the human slave trade was a booming business.

Sid sent him his location and asked how soon Teague could get there with a transponder, knowing full well it would take longer than he had, but hoping against hope he might be close by.

Papa isn't going to be happy if he finds out you're working on your vacation. I'm fifteen minutes out and leaving now.

Sid doubted Hackman would stick around that long. As for 'Papa', Teague's nickname for his father-in-law, the partially retired agency chief, he already knew there would be hell to pay. Sid had been Patrick Donley's personal assistant until Donley had stepped down. Though Papa was mostly retired, he worked as hard as he ever had. Instead of running the entire region, he now oversaw his local office only. He still had his fingers in all the important pies and still held an agent's career in the palm of his hand. One word from 'Papa' and your next assignment would make Siberia look inviting.

Several times Hackman glanced right at Sid. Each time Sid tensed, preparing for the worst, but Hackman merely continued going through the boxes.

While Hackman ransacked Sasha's storage unit, Sid tried to plan out his next move. Sasha was bound to leave town as soon as she knew her unit had been discovered.

After finding the lockbox, Hackman took a few moments to pick the lock and scavenge through the contents. Sid couldn't get a good look, but he watched Hackman pocket what looked like a photo.

In less than ten minutes, Hackman had searched the boxes and left, sliding the door down behind him. Sid waited a few minutes then climbed out from his hiding place. As soon as he hit the floor, he heard the telltale scraping sound of the door rolling up. He lay on the ground and scooted as far into the shadows as possible.

Moving slowly to keep his clothing from making any rustling sound, he reached behind his back and pulled his Sig Sauer from its holster. At the sound of liquid hitting the concrete floor he froze. Adrenaline flooded his body as the loud *whoosh* alerted him to the fire. The roar of flames drowned out the receding footsteps. Panic hit him like a punch to the gut as the door rolled shut.

A wall of flames blocked his only exit. The blaze seared his eyes as the soot clogged his airways. By the time he got the door up, he'd be fried to a crisp. Staying put wasn't an option either. He searched in vain for a sprinkler system. If the place had one, he couldn't see it, blinded as he was from the flames. He ripped his shirt off to cover his face and hands as the door rolled upward. Hackman was back.

The fresh air fueled the fire, causing another flare-up. Instinctively, he threw himself backward, hitting his head on the shelving. As he raised the pistol to shoot his way past Hackman, his vision faded to black.

* * * *

The pounding in his head, exacerbated by the sirens, told him he was in fact still alive. As consciousness crept back in, he was determined to get the hell out of there. Forcing his body into an upright position was harder than expected. Hands appeared from every direction to hold him down. Fear had him fighting like a crazy man. He refused to burn to death.

"Sid, you asshole, you pop me in the mouth again and I'm hitting back." Teague's booming voice pierced the veil of adrenaline-laced terror.

"That was for the one you thought you'd got away with," Sid croaked through his scorched throat.

"Keep that over your mouth and nose, sir," a paramedic advised him as he placed an oxygen mask over his face.

Gladly, he took several well-needed breaths. His lungs, parched from the heat and soot, couldn't handle the clean air and he began to cough.

As soon as his brain began to function again, he pulled the mask away. "You said Hackman was East Coast?"

"Born and raised," Teague confirmed.

Sid let go a slew of expletives. "He's here to acquire Sasha." He scrambled to his feet. Moving brought a fresh round of pain, but his only thought was of Sasha. Hackman had at least a ten minute head start.

He took several deep breaths to stave off the pain. It caused another round of coughing he couldn't avoid, though he scarcely had the time. After he was convinced his lungs weren't going to push past his teeth, he managed to catch enough breath to speak. "Did you see anyone leaving as you pulled up?"

"A white 2011 Chevy Express van."

"Did you get the plate?" Sid spared a glance at his friend.

"Of course I got the plate, when have I ever let you down?"

"Don't go there, if you hadn't stopped to play patty-cake with Chantel you'd have gotten here before the weenie roast."

"You're not a weenie. A little candy-assed on occasion, but not a weenie, and for all the drama you were barely singed."

Sid flipped him off as they climbed into the car. "Get a black and white over to Sasha's Designs in Paradise Valley." He rattled off the address from memory. "Detain Hackman until we can get there."

While Teague made the necessary arrangements, Sid called Sasha's office. "Hi, Cheryl, this is Jacob Erkins." He paused, giving a quiet, self-deprecating chuckle. "This is a bit embarrassing... I think I left my iPad there. Have you seen it?"

"No, I'm sorry I haven't," Cheryl answered, sounding worried for him.

"Could you ask Sasha if I left it in her office?"

When Sid bounced up over the median, Teague reached behind him to grab and buckle his seatbelt.

"She isn't here at the moment, but I'll check once she comes in," Cheryl responded.

"Oh, I see. When do you expect her back?"

Teague lunged forward to grab the wheel as Sid steered with his leg while reaching into the back for his laptop.

"I'm not sure. She had an offsite meeting. I can ask her to call you."

"No, there's no need. I'll just get it tomorrow. Thank you, Cheryl."

Sid pulled onto the sidewalk and stopped while he booted his laptop.

Teague reached over, killed the ignition and pocketed the keys. "What the hell are you doing?"

"Hackman has to be here to acquire or kill Sasha. She isn't at her office. Cheryl, her secretary, said she's at a business meeting. I'm trying to get a GPS read off her truck."

"I take it you've found her. Is she a suspect or a victim?"

"Give me the keys. I've got a lock on her."

"Sid, look around. We are sitting on the sidewalk in the middle of Old Town Scottsdale. I think you left your bumper on the median back there. I'll drive." Teague opened the passenger door and walked around to the driver's side.

Normally, Sid would never have allowed anyone to drive his baby, but time was of the essence and no one could argue like Teague. Sid crawled over the console to the passenger seat. "She's at the Tovrea Castle. Get on the 101."

Teague's cell phone rang as he was pulling into traffic. "Brody," he answered as he moved into the right lane and stepped on it. "All right," he sighed then slowed down.

"What are you doing?" Sid demanded.

"Hackman was in the alley about a block or so away from Sasha's Designs. When the black and white approached, he bolted. Use your head, man. If he was waiting behind her office, chances are he doesn't know where she is."

"You can't be sure of that. We need to get to the Tovrea Castle."

Teague reached over and pulled down the passenger vanity mirror. "Do you really intend to barge into her business meeting, *Jacob,* looking like that?"

His reflection startled him. His hair was singed on the ends. Soot smudges covered his face. His shirt was MIA. *Son of a bitch.* "Get one of *our* guys on her. Maybe Jeff or Dave. Someone good." He sent Teague the GPS data as well as her car's and personal description.

"Papa's gonna expect a report." Teague looked at Sid with compassion.

"Stall him. I need more time to figure this out," he answered without looking up from his computer.

"It doesn't work that way, Sid. The chief isn't going to buy the bullshit. You need to talk to him. Fill him in on what's going on." He pulled the car onto the freeway and headed toward the Tovrea Castle.

"Her truck is parked on the lower level. She knows this car so we need to find a vantage point away from walkways."

"I know the drill, Sid. Drop the closed mouth, close to the vest shit and tell me what you've learned," Teague demanded.

"Look, there's her truck." Sid pointed toward the vehicle. He wasn't ready to share this case with anyone else. He needed help and knew full well it would come with a price tag. He had to be very careful, though. Frankly, he didn't care what it cost him, but he didn't want Sasha to be part of the deal.

Every logical fiber in his brain told him Sasha was Alexa Desman, a three time murderess living on the run. Further south, either his gut or his dick, he couldn't be sure which, agreed that Sasha was Alexa Desman, but was fairly certain she couldn't murder a fly let alone three people. Unfortunately, the chief would rely on the evidence and the evidence all pointed to her guilt.

Teague found the perfect place to sit and wait. They could see both the most likely door she would exit from and her car. Sid knew his brief reprieve was over.

He took a deep breath, coughed, then laid out all facts, but he was careful to keep his personal feelings to himself.

"If that was all there was to it, you'd have her in custody and a hard-ass like Hackman wouldn't have her in his sights. So, what aren't you telling me?"

"Dave is coming around behind us. Pull forward."

"Don't think this is over," Teague grumbled as he moved the car forward.

Chapter Five

The water was heaven on earth as he washed off the soot and smoke. What could he tell Teague and his superiors that made sense? Sasha's prints had been on the designer's body, and the bloody prints on the murder weapon were pretty damning evidence. All he had to combat that were her animal rights activities and his own gut feelings.

Once Sid had dried off and put on a fresh suit, he found Teague sitting at his computer going through his encrypted files. "So much for privacy…"

"You're using an antiquated program, therefore you have no valid expectation of privacy," Teague retorted.

"Hack to your heart's content, I'm going to relieve Dave."

"Not without me," Teague reminded him, already shutting down the computer. "And I'm driving."

Sid booted his laptop as soon as he buckled up. "She's on the move. Back to her office, I suspect. Swing by and get your car. I'll watch the back while you watch the front. Once we're in place, cut Dave loose."

"Aye-aye, boss," Teague responded sarcastically.

* * * *

"What's she like?" Teague asked from his position in front of Sasha's business.

Sid kept his opinions to a minimum. "According to the IRS records she is highly successful. Her business has attracted the rich and famous. She has an air of mystery to her reputation. Yet she lives like a pauper. Her one-room apartment is in a seedy part of town. She has no debt, pays her bills in cash or from her business account, often in six month increments."

"Cold, elusive, lives bare-bones. What's her passion?" Teague cut through the crap.

Sid was glad they were a block apart with no visual available. He wasn't sure his face had remained neutral hearing Teague's summary. Sasha was far from cold. She was sunshine on a dreary day. As sappy as that sounded, it was the truth. He was fucked. Either she was a killer or she had a professional killer stalking her. One thing was sure, life was never boring.

"Animals, horses primarily. She donates a significant amount of her time and artwork to a local horse rescue."

"Have you found any connection to the East Coast? Is she smuggling for them? Money laundering?"

"Not that I've discovered." Truth is he hadn't looked, but he should have. He'd lost count of the mistakes he'd made on this case. He was lucky he wasn't dead. Mistakes were often deadly in his business. He had a lead reminder in his head. He certainly knew better.

"The crime scene photos were pretty gruesome when you consider a tween was the doer."

Sid knew Teague was baiting him and he refused to give any more away.

"You banging her, *Jacob*?"

"Shut the fuck up, Teague."

"Cuz that would be really stupid, man."

"This from the guy who was 'banging' the chief's only daughter, while eluding Mr. G's henchmen, a serial killer and a rogue agent. Fuck you, Teague. Don't talk to me about stupid."

"Not so stupid, I came away with a beautiful bride, a six-figure reward and a very powerful father-in-law who thinks the sun rises and sets because of me," Teague gloated.

"You got really lucky, man. How you didn't end up dead or in jail still baffles my mind." And at times like this pissed him off.

"No luck required when you got skill. Now, banging a murderess? That's ballsy. Sid would never consider such a foolhardy maneuver. *Jacob* must like to live on the edge."

"I didn't say I was banging her. Your mind is always on sex. You think with your dick. How many times did that almost get you killed?"

"Doesn't matter. I'm still alive and kickin'. And Channy is the only one I think about like that now, so don't go there."

"Sasha's not a killer." Sid could not believe he spoke those words out loud, or even thought them. The idea of Sasha in Hackman's hands tied his guts into knots. They had to make sure they found her before Hackman did.

"I feel the need to point out the only prints on the murder weapon and the dead girl belonged to your love muffin."

"Knock it off, Teague. I'm well aware she's a murder suspect. Keep in mind, she also has a straight-up killer searching for her."

"Putting all that aside, let's say she didn't do it. When this all washes out, and she finds out you're a Fed, how will she deal with the deception?"

"I'll cross that bridge when I get there." Teague wasn't helping. Sid knew he was fucked. To keep her safe he had to lock her up, let her run or stick to her like glue. It was crazy to actually believe he had developed sincere emotions for her. Wasn't it? He didn't know anything anymore. Nothing added up. "She's coming out the back. If she follows her normal routine, she's headed to dinner."

"How long you been tailing her?" Teague asked casually.

Sid wasn't fooled. "I know where she's headed. Thanks for the help tonight."

"Sid, there's no way I can just drive off and let this drop."

"I don't expect you to. File your report. Fill in the chief. I knew when I called for help the can I was opening." Sid would never ask a friend to stick his neck out for him. Some part of him was disappointed though.

"You jackass. This isn't about policy violations and everything to do with you risking your life." His anger and frustration was evident in his voice.

"Do what you have to do, Teague. I'm going to try and meet her at the restaurant. We can't keep her safe a block away." He tore off, breaking every speed limit. For this to work, he needed to get there ahead of her.

"You're assuming she's in danger. What if she's part of their organization?"

Sid didn't want to hear or think about the possibility that Hackman was the boyfriend she'd told the police about. "She could be, but you don't set fire to someone's property to stay in their good graces. If there is such a connection, we may be able to use that to our advantage." He scanned the parking lot but didn't see her car. He hoped she hadn't deviated from her routine.

"She may not know she's become expendable. Use your head, Sid. You could be walking into a very hostile situation."

"I hear ya." He grabbed his laptop and headed into the restaurant with a lot more confidence than he really felt. What was the difference between assertive and a creeper? If he crossed the line, she would disappear. With Hackman in the area, he was running out of time.

It was late in the evening and the hostess area was empty, which was perfect for *Jacob*. He didn't want to be seated until he had a chance to catch up to Sasha. To be on the safe side, he stood in the shadows, hoping not to draw the attention of an employee. He didn't wait long before Sasha came through the lobby.

Sid stayed hidden until she was away from the door. "Sasha, I was hoping I would run into you!" Afraid she would turn and walk out, he placed his body between her and the exit.

Sasha had half turned to leave, when she stopped and stared at his face. "Oh my goodness, what happened to you?" Her concern apparently overruled her good judgment.

His hand came up to touch his seared face. With a chagrinned expression, he wove another tale of lies. "My client this afternoon wanted to meet poolside. While I sat baking my brains out, he was swimming laps."

Finally Roberto showed up and saved him from further deception. "Ms. Sasha, you brought your young man back to see us. I have just the table. Come with me."

Sasha didn't know what to say so she said nothing as Roberto led them to a secluded table with a gorgeous view of the city lights. She slid into the booth and was pleased when he sat beside her. "Why did you put up with it?"

With a casual shrug, he explained, "I'm paid by the hour. If he wants to pay me to watch him swim laps, I'm fine with that. Besides, it gave me time to work on your sites."

"What are you talking about?" She turned slightly sideways so she could watch his expressions.

Jacob closed the distance between them and brought up her company's page on his laptop. "Your website isn't very secure."

As their thighs touched her breath caught in her throat. An image of him looming above her as his knee parted her legs flashed in her mind, almost causing her to moan. She desperately pushed those thoughts aside. She needed to watch what he was showing her.

"With just a few keystrokes I was able to obtain administrator access. If your personal data isn't better protected, you could run into some serious problems," Jacob informed her.

A more immediate problem was how to handle her attraction to Jacob. She rested her hand on his leg as she turned to point to a drop-down box on the screen. At the feel of his rock-hard muscles, her brain went a little fuzzy. She was getting in over her head and she needed to stop. Stop now. Sasha drew her hand back and scooted as far away from him as the booth would allow.

When she was sure she could speak with a normal voice instead of a breathy whisper, she explained, "I don't accept any type of payments over the Internet, so how damaging could it really be?"

"Sasha, a hacker could wipe you out." His voice was stern, as if she were a child being taken to task.

After a deep calming breath, she started thinking about the implications. "I don't see how. Just gaining access to my business website would be inconvenient, but it wouldn't give them access to my accounts. My records are all saved onto the hard drive at the office. Someone would have to steal my computer before they would be able to hack into my finances or personal data, right?" On one hand, she had hoped to send a virus or something to her brother's computer, enabling her to have access to his private files, but now that she considered how vulnerable her own systems might be, the hairs on the back of her neck began to tingle.

"Not necessarily. It only takes seconds to download a copy of the entire hard drive. If your secretary ran out for coffee, someone could hack your info and be gone without anyone being the wiser. There are even ways to monitor every keystroke made on a computer."

A sick feeling started to grow in the pit of her stomach. If someone found and hacked her financial accounts, it would effectively cut her wings and ruin her ability to escape. "They could access all my accounts and learn all my passwords?"

"Quite easily, I'm afraid," he acknowledged, but he softened the blow with a brush of his thumb along her cheek.

Her thoughts jumbled whenever he touched her, but she couldn't bring herself to pull away. "So it's not just my business that's in danger. Someone could easily steal my identity. That's what you meant when you said wipe me out. They could empty my accounts, encumber debt…anything." Unease had blossomed into panic.

Sid watched the color drain from Sasha's face. Was there more going on than Sasha simply covering her back trail? Now he kicked himself for not checking out the data from her laptop. While his curiosity was piqued, it would have to wait until he was alone.

"I could look at it, if you want me to," he offered casually. "It would only take a few minutes." His brain started examining the situation from all the angles. If she was as concerned as she appeared, he could use this to his advantage.

"Now that you've showed me how easy it is, I'm getting a little worried. Someone broke into the office a few weeks ago. I never keep any sizable amounts money there, but thieves wouldn't know that. I'd assumed they'd broken in looking for cash. When they didn't find any, they tossed the furniture around and left. Now I'm wondering if they might have been after something else."

The sweet taste of triumph surged through him. She had told the police her boyfriend had ransacked the office after an argument then refused to give his name. While he had doubted the truth of that story, once Hackman had entered the picture he had been afraid it might be true. The thought of Hackman and Sasha together made Sid's stomach roll. Hackman was a dangerous, sadistic man.

"After dinner, we can run by your place. I can easily check to see if the system has been compromised and download a software program that will make it much more complicated to breach the firewall."

Once they were back at her office, he could easily keep her there most of the night. He could run system scans that would take hours. Maybe he'd even test out his charm and see where that might lead them. The mere thought had his cock jumping to life.

"Are you sure you don't mind? I hate to take up your evening. It's already quite late."

She seemed anxious.

"I don't sleep much. Most nights I either workout or waste time on the computer. It would be nice to have such beautiful company for a change. If you need to get home though, we can do it another day." He knew it was a gamble to offer, but he couldn't afford to sound too eager. She was suspicious of everything and everyone. Given a few minutes, she might decide he was trying to scam her and suddenly change her mind. He still hadn't forgotten the disappearing act she'd pulled the other night in the same restaurant.

"I'm an insomniac too. This business is my livelihood and I seem to do my best creative thinking in the wee hours."

Damn, her shy smile sent a jolt of electricity straight to his dick. Teague's words whirled around in his mind, tempering his raging lust. Once this mess was cleared up, how would she react to his deception? Not well, he feared.

"Another thing we have in common. This may be fate, Ms. Sasha."

Sid was pretty sure he was getting underneath the first layer of her armor. He noticed a slight change in her facial expression. A very subtle squint then a downward cast of her eyes told him his comment made her unhappy. Sadness radiated from her. So much so, he felt compelled to take it away. He was finding it harder and harder to keep up the façade. If his suspicions were correct, she had been dealt a lousy hand indeed.

This time dinner lacked those awkward moments. They laughed and talked like old friends. Sid was given further proof that he was making headway with Sasha when she agreed to ride with him. Once he parked outside her shop, he took a slow, careful look around. With few cars on the road, he was reasonably sure no one had followed them, but it was impossible to evade a would-be tail without it raising Sasha's suspicions. At the door, as she dug through her purse to find her keys, he shielded her as best he could without it being obvious.

Sasha immediately locked it again behind them. "I have two desktops and a laptop. My receptionist has some access, but it's very limited." Her tone was clipped and businesslike.

He breathed a sigh of relief once they were both safely inside, but her sudden change in demeanor left him unsettled. "Were all three here when you had the break-in?"

"Yes, I'm not much of a computer person. I take my laptop to client meetings, more because it is expected than to serve an actual purpose." She was skirting the truth.

Sid booted his computer, linking it with the receptionist's desktop. "Do you know Cheryl's password? I can work around it, but it will be quicker if you know it."

Shock skittered across her face. "You shouldn't need a password. Why is it password-protected? I specifically had this computer set up with limited access so passwords and security wouldn't be needed."

Sid knew Sasha had to be worried Cheryl was up to something. "It isn't a big deal. I can override it."

"Yes, override it. Can you find out what she's been doing on this computer? It is company property. She signed a waiver voiding any right to privacy." Her mind seemed to be whirling.

He watched Sasha pace across the floor. She seemed more frightened than angry, though there was a hint of fire across her cheeks. She looked sexy as hell. "It shouldn't be a problem." He buried his smile. This was perfect. Now she wouldn't be suspicious of him when he took longer than expected.

"Let me get this software running and we can go into your office and check out the other computers." He wanted them away from the windows. With the lights blazing they were on display.

Sasha unlocked her office. Based on the clicking of the keyboards, he assumed she'd booted them and entered the passwords for each.

As Sid finished up at Cheryl's desk, he watched Sasha out of the corner of his eye.

Her agitation was eating at him. The pacing and wringing her hands together had the tension level spiked. What surprised him most though was his reaction to her distress. His stomach tightened into knots.

Sid joined Sasha in her office. He sat down and patted the settee next to him, a silent command for her to join him. "This is going to take a while, Sasha. Come and sit down. I'm offering a free shoulder massage this week to all stressed-out business owners."

She slowed down and looked at him with wide, haunted eyes.

"No waiting," he encouraged her further.

Hesitantly, she walked across the room. For a brief moment their gazes locked. Her expression softened as she turned away and sat with her back to him.

With his palms on her shoulders he could feel the knots in her muscles. Slowly he began to massage them away. At first she remained rigid, her back ramrod straight as she stared straight ahead. A few moments later, as he swirled his thumbs along her neck, she began to coo and moan.

Sid was pretty sure she had no idea her sexy as hell sounds sent a shot of rock-hard straight to his cock. Obviously the sudden rush of blood to lower regions of his anatomy blocked all moral and ethical thought processes, allowing instinct to take over. As she leaned back into him, he skimmed his lips down her neck. So feminine...he couldn't have pulled away if she'd insisted. Proving once again that God had a soft spot for fools, Sasha tilted her head a little more, allowing him greater access to her deliciously soft skin.

"You should advertise this sale. You'd have customers lined up for miles," she whispered to him.

Her voice, husky and low, had him straining the fabric of his pants. She was torturing him one breathy expression at a time. He was afraid to move too fast. Sasha always had one foot out of the door. Yet if he didn't get relief soon, he might embarrass himself.

"This promotion is only available to very special customers. In fact, I know of only one that qualifies."

"I wish I'd hired you long ago." Sasha spoke quietly.

"My thoughts exactly." Male satisfaction rang clear in his voice. Her fingers weren't the only thing she had twisted into knots. Every muscle in her body was stretched taut. He was amazed she was allowing his touch. Still, he wanted more. So much more. Did he dare?

Slowly the tension eased, her heart beat a strong, steady rhythm. "Lay down on your stomach," he whispered in her ear as he nibbled down her neck.

For several seconds she froze in place. Looking over her shoulder, she met his gaze. With a consensual nod, she stretched forward onto her tummy, a languid cat allowing her master to pet her. The random thought wreaked havoc with his control.

He'd noticed her elegant feline-like movements during his surveillance and recognized her enemy potential. Her lean physique had muscles toned to give her both speed and endurance in a fight. If she was trained in martial arts, as he suspected, she was a dangerous and potentially deadly opponent.

Now that he'd gotten to know her and realized her abhorrence to violence, those smooth, controlled movements pushed all his sexual buttons.

Slowly, giving her time to object, he inched her shirt to her shoulders, exposing more of her intoxicating skin. She had a nasty bruise, presumably from the fall while riding. Though considering her evening adventures and backward falls from a second story window, it was anyone's guess where it had come from. The urge to shake some sense into her nearly overrode his need to kiss her pain away.

They were quite the pair. He with his singed hair and burnt face. Sasha with her broken wrist and assorted bruises. Both cloaked in layers of lies. Sid wondered how she'd react once she learned the truth about him. And he was pretty convinced it was a matter of when, not if.

He was afraid to speak and slip out of character or say the wrong thing and ruin this perfect moment so he let his lips caress the angry blue-black mar spanning most of her ribcage. As his hands cupped her narrow waist, a primitive need to protect her nearly swamped him. She was so small and fragile. What the hell had happened in her life to have her living in a drug and crime-infested part of town, with a sanctioned mob hitman stalking her? He kept his movements slow, half expecting her to stop him at any moment.

"Oh, Jacob, that feels wonderful."

A sour taste began to grow in his mouth. Sid Townsend wanted to be the one touching, her not Jacob Erkins. *Damn it. Just damn it all.*

Chapter Six

After seeing a couple of cops near Sasha's office, Hackman decided to try to catch his prey at the restaurant Desman had told him she frequented. He was surprised to see her leave with a man. Most of the women he'd retrieved over the years avoided anyone with a dick. Quickly he jotted down the license plate number, year and make of the car the man was driving. Something was very odd about this retrieval. Since he didn't trust Desman as far as he could throw the bastard, Hackman needed as much information he could get. Soon, he'd know all about the man and just how much of an inconvenience he would turn out to be. Hackman wasn't leaving any loose ends on this job.

Once the parking lot cleared out, he pulled his van behind the trunk of the woman's car. In seconds flat, he'd jimmied the lock and begun a thorough search. Beyond swashes of fabric and paint chips, he found little else. Yet pieces of a puzzle were beginning to come together. The hairs on the back of his neck were standing on end. He usually didn't care who he accepted a job from or what the end result would eventually be for his target, but Desman rubbed him the wrong way. He would sell out his own mother.

It only took one phone call to an associate in the police department to get the address and employer of the man driving away with Hackman's target. He wasn't surprised to learn the man was federal government worker, aka a Fed. He might not be able to determine which law enforcement department he worked for, but it was becoming obvious the cops were involved in this mess.

The urge to shove it down Desman's throat was strong. Still, Hackman hadn't stayed alive this long by being careless and going off half-cocked. He placed a tracking device on the woman's car then used Google Maps to look up the address for the Fed. He would include a visit to the man's apartment in his list of stops to make that evening.

* * * *

"Sasha, where do you see yourself in five years?" A war raged inside Sid's mind. He'd felt her surrender. If he'd kept his mouth shut, he'd be well on his way to making sweet love to her. Well, Jacob would have. Instead, he felt her muscles tense and she pushed her torso off the couch. "Easy now," he whispered near her ear.

"Such a somber question, Jacob." Sasha turned her face away, but eased back onto the cushions. "I expect I'll be working day and night trying to stay afloat."

"Is that all you want out of life? A successful business?" His hands never faltered. As he massaged her knotted muscles, he felt her heart rate rise. It appeared discussing their future plans upset Sasha.

"Well, a girl has gotta eat and I have my employees to think about too. If I don't bring in the money, a lot of people will have to scramble to make ends meet."

Sid knew that was another lie and noticed that once again she'd twirled her earring. It looked like a reliable tell. "Do you see yourself in a relationship?"

"No. I don't think that's in the cards for me." She sounded very sure of herself.

"You're a young woman, Sasha. Why are you ruling out the whole two point five kids and the white picket fence?" He slid his hands farther down her back to the swell of her gorgeous ass.

She turned the dainty stud in her ear one more time. "I'm a career girl. The whole husband, kid thing just doesn't do it for me."

"One day, far, far from now, I think I'd like to give it a try. I can't say I'm in a hurry though. My focus right now needs to be on work. Maybe in a few years I'll be in a position to settle down." He felt her relax again.

"Until then you're just going to play the field and enjoy bachelorhood?" She sounded flirty and playful again.

"I wouldn't mind finding a friend with benefits. I'm not really the bar hopping, one-night stand type." He hoped he was playing it right.

"I'm not either. My last relationship didn't end well and I've avoided dating since then."

His hands kneaded her perfectly shaped and toned ass while his mind considered several deliciously naughty things he'd rather be doing to it. Damn, he couldn't remember the last time he'd been laid. Jumping in the sack with a murder suspect was definitely one of his less intelligent ideas, but he was finding it hard to think of her that way. "How long ago was that?"

She hesitated a moment, but eventually answered. "About three years ago."

Sid kept one hand on her ass, but leaned down near her face. "High five, you actually beat me in the celibacy race, and I figured that was hard to do. I'm coming up on two years."

A smile broke across her face and she slapped his hand with hers. "What do you say? Should we start the clock over?" Her face turned a lovely shade of red, as if the question had slipped out.

Sid paused a moment and considered his next move. "Are you offering me a friends with benefits style arrangement?"

She slid her face below her arm, but he could see she was embarrassed and intrigued at the offer.

"I've never done anything like that. How would it work?" she asked without looking at him.

"We can discuss the parameters and make sure it suits both our needs. What would work for you?" He couldn't make it too easy or she'd get spooked. He needed to make sure some of his desires were addressed as well. Hell, who was he kidding? This is what he'd wanted and been angling toward since he'd first laid eyes on her.

"I miss being hugged."

He could hear the tears in her voice and his doubts fell away. The mission fell away. Sid pulled her into his arms. Holding her tightly, he felt a peace wash over him. "I miss it too. Physical contact is important. I'm so careful to avoid giving a woman the wrong impression that I tend to avoid intimate situations entirely."

Her head, which had been nestled against his shoulder, tipped upward, allowing him to see her eyes. Some emotion passed across her face and he wondered what she was thinking.

"You don't want to get a woman's hopes up?" She smiled and settled back against his shoulder. "Not to worry. I'm not waiting for my knight in shining armor to ride in and carry me off to a house full of kids and a white picket fence."

"That helps."

"But?" She sounded unsure.

He grinned nervously as he decided to share a real piece of himself. "Would you believe I like my sex a bit on the kinky side?" This was always a tough conversation to have with a woman. He was shocked how many acted like he was a social pariah and needed to be locked up.

She tilted her head back and looked at him, her expression comical. Evidently he'd shocked her.

"Don't take this wrong, but no, you don't seem the 'get down and dirty' type."

Everyone kidded him about his 'uptight' nature. He wasn't surprised she'd picked up on it too. "Would you believe I'm a control freak?"

"Now that I do believe, but unlike some people I think you use it to your advantage. You've used those traits to enhance your life rather than allow them to detract from it." She was finger tracing circles on the part of his chest peeking out of his shirt.

Her summation of him was a little startling. She was highly intuitive and that was dangerous in his line of work. It made sense though. Living on the run, sometimes on the street, she'd had to develop a skill set that kept her safe, and part of that was reading people.

"What gave me away?" He was curious about her thinking process and if he had tells he wasn't aware of.

"You're confident without being arrogant. You're relaxed in your own skin. That's a pretty rare trait and...one I find particularly appealing." She hid her face a little deeper in his shoulder.

He loved that she was willing to go outside her comfort zone for him. "What else?"

"You pay attention to details. Your clothes are always immaculate, but you don't stress over them. I've never caught you checking a mirror or straightening your shirt. That tells me you strive to be your best, but you don't obsess over perfection." She stopped making circles then began again in the other direction. "What I don't understand is how that correlates to sex."

"You described me pretty well. Let's see if I can do the same for you. Since you own your own business, you make decisions all day long. You're in control of every aspect. Your brain is constantly working on something. It never shuts off or gives you a break."

Sasha looked intrigued as she nodded.

"Do you ever wish you could lay it all down for a while and let someone else take charge?" When she started to protest, he quickly clarified. "Not of your business or your professional life, but of your body and your sexual needs. I think you'd like someone— No, not just anyone..." He needed to take this discussion out of the hypothetical and make it more personal. "I think you'd like *me* to step in and quiet that busy mind of yours, to give you an evening's reprieve from thinking and stressing."

"Sounds heavenly, but also impossible. You may have noticed I have some trust issues." She laughed, but it was obviously forced.

"What if you approved of everything ahead of time?" Her beautiful face was flushed and her breathing quick and shallow. He'd suspected she was submissive.

"It sounds like the death of spontaneity." She spoke softly, as if she were afraid she'd offend him.

He smiled, knowing he had her now. "You're a designer...if five customers approached you and said they each wanted a room decorated in muted earth tones, would all their rooms be the same?"

"Of course not. There are thousands of variations and com-bin-ations." She spread the last word out as realization seemed to dawn on her. "I see what you're saying." She sighed. She tipped her head from side to side as if she wasn't convinced.

"But?"

"But, I'm not sure I'm capable of letting anyone else be in charge."

"Let's try a few things. If you become too uncomfortable just say stop and I will."

She drew back away from him and crossed her arms in front of her.

"The funny thing about trust is you have to give a little bit" — he held up his thumb and index finger about an inch apart— "in order for more to be earned. Trust is gained slowly, over time and through experiences. I haven't done anything to earn your trust, but if you'll give me a little leeway, maybe I can."

He was wrong. He'd done a few things to earn her trust. When she'd gotten into a vehicle with him, he hadn't knocked her out and handed her over to the sex-slave ring. That definitely earned him a few points. She was here alone with him and he hadn't done anything she hadn't wanted or hadn't enjoyed. "Okay. But I'll warn you, I have the word 'stop' on speed dial. Don't be hurt if I whip it out there."

Jacob laughed like she'd hoped he would.

"You won't hurt my feelings, but I'll be disappointed. I want to be what you need. Let me ask you something. You are a very sensual woman. I get aroused just watching you. When you were with your previous boyfriend, was sex something you looked forward to?"

What a question. She wasn't sure how to answer. She enjoyed being held afterward. "Sh-sure."

"Tsk, tsk, Sasha. I don't know if you're lying to just me or to both of us, but that was certainly not the truth." He tipped her chin upward and met her gaze.

The word stop was on the tip of her tongue. She didn't like being called on her actions. He was wanting a real piece of her. He wasn't going to be satisfied with a carefully manicured façade. The idea was frightening.

When had she become such a coward? A conversation couldn't hurt her. Her face was flaming hot with embarrassment. "It wasn't a complete lie. I looked forward to cuddling."

"Did you orgasm from intercourse?" he asked calmly, as if inquiring about the time of day.

"Not usually, but it doesn't matter. Orgasms aren't all that important to me." It was unrealistic to think they'd happen every time. She'd read somewhere that not every woman could climax from intercourse alone. Chances were good she was one of the unlucky few.

"Do you come when you masturbate?" He kissed her forehead.

Oh, no. She wasn't going to answer that. "That's a horrible question. If I say no, then something's wrong with me. If I say yes, I'm admitting to playing with myself. I think I'll pass." She waved her fingers as if that would force the conversation to keep flowing. "Move on."

His eyes bored into her, lighting her blood on fire. Holy hell, he was potent.

"Not a chance, Sasha. Remember, I'm in charge now. You're letting me decide what information I need to make our time together special."

She felt vulnerable and it was hard to breathe, but she didn't want it to stop. The funny feeling she had in the pit of her stomach, the warmth and tingling, spread lower.

"There's no shame in taking care of your needs, Sasha. Heaven knows I've taken matters into my own hands more than a few times."

Having him admit it first made it easier. "I try not to think about it too much." Masturbating only reminded her how lonely she was.

"Answer my question, Sasha."

"Yes," she hissed in a fit of temper.

He smiled. "Thank you. I'm what's called a service top. Have you ever heard the term?"

"I have no idea what you're talking about. What's a top...other than a child's toy or a blouse?" She giggled nervously.

"It just means that I'm a Dominant who enjoys taking caring of my submissive partner," he explained patiently.

"But I'm not submissive."

"Is it possible that you are, but you've never had the opportunity to explore that side of your personality?"

She shrugged. "I've learned that anything is possible."

"Have you ever been spanked?" He shot her a playful grin that sent heat straight to her clit.

"No." But she had read plenty of novels where the heroine found it enjoyable. She'd always thought that the author had taken artistic license with those scenes, but she might be willing to give it a try...just once.

"But you're curious?"

His voice took on that low and seductive note she enjoyed hearing so much. She nodded.

"Not good enough, my sweet. I want to hear your answers out loud." His tone changed just the slightest bit to take on an edge.

"Yes, I'm a little curious." And that was the most she was saying on that subject.

"Good to know." He ran a finger down her cheek before pulling on her blouse. "Get rid of this."

What? One look and she knew she hadn't heard him wrong. It was time to decide. Was she going to let fear take away her chance of a special evening or was she going to be strong and see this through? Slowly, she drew the shirt over her head. As the cool air hit her body, her daring faded. She crumpled her blouse in her lap, refusing to look at Jacob.

"Thank you. That took guts. It's hard being bare in front of another person, especially while they're still dressed. You're feeling exposed, aren't you?" He ran his hand down her back.

She nodded. It *was* worse with him completely dressed. Hot, though, too.

"I like your fire, Sasha. You're such a brave woman and with strong convictions. I love how you quietly crusade for abused animals. Most people toss a few dollars their way and pat themselves on the back for being such a do-gooder."

His praise touched her. He might not mean any of it. He might just be playing her to get the arrangement he wanted, but he sounded sincere.

She folded her shirt and tossed it onto the coffee table, but kept her gaze lowered.

"Take off your bra."

Though she'd been expecting the command, her stomach plummeted. "Not yet." She stole a glance his way.

His eyes twinkled and she could see she'd surprised him. Hell, the whole evening thus far had shocked her so he could just join the club.

"Why are you hesitating?"

What the hell? He wanted her to tell him what she was thinking about? No. It would be easier to take the damn thing off than to talk about why she didn't want to. Maybe she could bluff her way through this. She lifted her cast-covered arm. "Could you help me?"

From his raised eyebrow and quirked smile, she knew she hadn't fooled him. Still, he unsnapped her bra without calling her on it. She'd take that as a small victory.

With her good hand, she slid the straps down her arms. After taking a deep breath, she pulled the silky fabric away from her breasts and placed it on top of her shirt.

Jacob didn't say a word, he simply watched her. His gaze felt as intimate as a caress. Her nipples hardened as she waited.

She wanted this. If she kept that foremost in her mind, maybe she'd find the guts to follow through. After drawing a slow, calming breath, she took stock of her body. Her panties were wet and he hadn't really touched her. How was she going to hide that fact from him? She shifted on his lap and felt his cock pressing into her hip. Instantly she stilled, causing Jacob to laugh.

"Wouldn't you be upset if I was unaffected? After all, you are sitting topless on my lap."

The whole situation was more than she could fathom. Her giggles bubbled over and she wrapped her arms around his neck for support. "Yeah, I guess I would be."

He held her for a few moments then pulled far enough away that she could see his face. His expression had changed. There was a seriousness that hadn't been there before. His gaze was direct and unwavering. Holy shit, he was killing her.

"Stand up, take off your skirt and panties. Fold and add them to the pile."

It was getting hard to breathe again. She didn't know if she had the guts to do this. What would he ask of her next?

Digging past the fear, she knew she wanted to find out. Slowly, she stood and followed his orders. She tucked her drenched panties inside her skirt. Butterflies were alive and in flight in her stomach.

"Kneel and link your hands behind your back," Jacob ordered. He slid one finger down the side of her cheek. "You're beautiful and you know it, but I suspect you wish people wouldn't notice." He tipped his head and looked deep in thought.

"You're savvy though. You know that beauty opens doors, so you don't hide it. The clothes you choose are professional and understated. You've chosen not to highlight your ample assets." His hand traveled the curve of her breast. "Why would that be, Sasha?"

He was seeing too much of her, the real her. Like a deer frozen by headlights, she didn't have the sense to run. It was probably too late anyway. He seemed to see straight through any façade she used.

"My designs have to be good enough to stand on their own. I don't want a job because someone wants to have sex with me."

"You say that like sex is a bad thing." He chuckled.

His smile softened his features and allowed her to relax a little. "It also helps gain some respect with my female clients," she confided.

"But they still hate you. They see you as competition and remain cold and a little bitchy." Jacob's voice was low yet filled with confidence in his assumptions.

He'd nailed it. "Are you sure you're not a closet shrink? You're very insightful."

"Reading people is a must in business...and as a Dom."

Just like that, he'd brought it full circle. Suddenly she was aware of the carpet fibers biting into her bare knees and the fact that he was still fully clothed. She'd never been in such a subservient position, and if asked, she would have sworn she never would be. Yet she had no desire to be anywhere else.

The look in Jacob's eyes intrigued her. There was approval. Such a simple thing, but she couldn't remember feeling it before. Maybe long ago, from her parents...

"Sex isn't a bad thing. It isn't something to be endured so you can snuggle afterward." His light friendly tone was gone, replaced by a strength he hadn't exhibited before this evening.

"I don't think it's bad, per se. You're twisting my words, making me sound like a prude."

"Then tell me how it is."

Her face grew hot. She tipped her head, hoping to hide her blushing. She should have known he'd start with the questions again. It was impossible to get her thoughts in order. Her brain was on overload as her body started a slow meltdown. His penetrating gaze was more potent than most men's touch.

"It's cheap." *Oh, crap.* Why had that come out of her mouth? Before she could scramble to her feet and get away, Jacob was down on his knees in front of her. He held her chin tenderly, keeping her from dodging his gaze.

"It doesn't have to be."

"Look at me. I'm like a cat in heat begging for your attention. It doesn't get much cheaper than that." Tears clogged her throat.

"The first time I saw you, I felt a connection. I don't believe in love at first sight and I know it isn't an emotion you want to discuss, but I knew we would click. I know I'm not the biggest Don Juan of our time, but believe it or not, I've had the opportunity to have sex a time or two within the last two years. I didn't choose to act on it. I have to like the woman, to feel a spark beyond mere lust, or it isn't worthy of my time and energy."

His words meant more to her than she'd imagined possible. A declaration of love would have sent her running, but knowing that he saw her as more than an easy lay mattered.

"Sex has felt superficial in the past because your needs weren't being met. Tonight, we're going to slow down those wheels turning in your head and show you there's more to intimacy than wham bam I'm outta here, ma'am."

A laugh bubbled up, surprising her. "Are you equating my brain to a gerbil?"

Chapter Seven

Sid fell back on his heels. He'd been convinced she was about to run and now she was teasing him. The more time he spent with her, the more he liked her.

Since her resolve seemed firmly back in place, it was time to get the scene moving. "I would never do such a thing." He gave her a kiss on her forehead before sliding back onto the couch. "Spread your legs to shoulder width."

Sasha's jaw tightened a moment before she followed his instruction. She was so beautiful. The image of her kneeling at his feet was forever engraved into his mind. He felt a great deal of pressure to make this evening something special for her, but how to do that without scaring her off was a quandary.

"Touch your pussy."

Her whole body flinched as if he'd struck her. "No, stop. I'm not doing this."

Before he could reach her, she was on her feet with her back to him. He circled her waist with his arm and pulled her back against him. He'd obviously hit a trigger of some sort. "What is it, Sasha? What's the matter?" he asked as he rubbed his chin in her hair.

She stood completely still, but she didn't pull away from him. "I'm not here for your entertainment. I'm not some sex doll you can watch perform while you jack off. I think you need to leave now." She turned and reached for her clothes.

Sid was getting a peek into her life that he hadn't expected. Her time on the run must have had some hellish points. Seeing the polished woman that stood before him, it was hard to always keep that in mind, especially when his cock was doing most of the thinking. "That is not what I wanted from you. Don't shut me out. Let me hold you in my arms and talk this through."

For a few scary seconds he figured he'd blown it, but then she started to relax her rigid muscles and he knew he'd won a second chance.

The stiff nod of her head was all he needed to see. He picked her up and carried her back to the couch. "I stumbled onto a shitty memory, didn't I?"

Sasha kept her head down, but confirmed his suspicions.

"We all have events in our lives we'd rather not revisit. I'm sorry I took you to a bad place. From your reaction, I know where you think I was headed. We haven't formed a layer of trust yet, so your mind is whirling, trying to stay one step ahead. As we spend more time together, it will get easier." He held her while his heart returned its normal rhythm. He'd hurt her, damn it. Until she was willing to share the intimate details of her life, he was flying blind.

"I overreacted. I'm sorry." Her voice was soft and husky, as if she were fighting to control her emotions.

"There's nothing to be sorry about. This is how trust is developed. Now I know if our play gets too intense, you'll make me aware of the situation and you now know that if you tell me to stop, I will. See, we're making progress."

"This doesn't feel much like progress, Jacob."

"Are we going to have a 'half full, half empty' conversation?" He kept his tone light, hoping she would relax.

"It's pointless, I guess."

"Far from it." He looked around her office. He needed something to work with. "Those swatches of cloth over there" — he pointed toward a chair near the window — "can I use those for a few minutes?"

She looked first at the cloth then at his face. "You can't tie me up. I'm sorry, it's not you. It's me. I have enough baggage to fill up an ocean liner. I wasn't kidding when I said I had trust issues."

Her face had paled and every ounce of tension was back in full force.

"Sasha, you are trying to anticipate my actions. You assumed I wanted you to play with yourself. I didn't. You assumed I was going to tie you up. That wasn't my plan. You told me you have trust issues and I heard you. I believe you." Sid continued to hold her, soothing them both.

"I'm sorry," she mumbled against his chest. "I don't know what you want from me."

"From the sound of things, your past experiences have been less than satisfying. I hope I'm not as predictable. Will you give me some leeway?"

"Are you sure it's worth all this trouble? I think I've embarrassed myself enough for one night." Sasha's voice was so soft he had to strain to hear her.

"Enough of that. Lay down on your back, arms over your head, legs slightly apart. If you'd like, you may close your eyes." He lifted her to her feet and gave her ass a sharp smack.

Her soft yelp made him chuckle. She'd shot him a dirty look, but heat had flared in her eyes as well. He didn't look at her as he walked to the window. It had to be her choice to follow his instructions.

Sifting through the pieces of fabric, he found several that would suit his purposes nicely. With more trepidation than he'd experienced before, he turned around. A sigh of relief escaped seeing Sasha lying on the rug as directed.

She had been watching his every move. The knowledge made him determined to win her trust. He dropped his bundle just above her hands, hopefully out of sight.

He drew a piece of lace from the pile. "I want to use this as a blindfold. If you need to, you'll be able to see through it. You'll know you're in no danger, but it will add a hint of mystery." Sid held his breath while she considered it. When she nodded, he felt as if he'd won a major concession.

Carefully, he slid the fabric under her head and made a simple square knot on the side so she was able to lie back comfortably. Since he wasn't the stop when you're ahead type, he decided to roll the dice once more. "Open your hands."

He wrapped another piece of cloth around her wrists, but put the ends into her palms. "I'm not going to tie this. You're going to hold it in place for me. If you needed to, you could easily get loose."

Watching her closely, he noticed her pulse beating wildly through the vein in her neck. As he placed his hand on her arm, she jumped. "You're doing fine,

Sasha. Take a deep breath and slowly let it go. You can do this. I'm not going to hurt you and if you need to stop just say so."

Once her shoulders sank a little deeper into the carpet, Sid ran a finger down the side of her breast. Her lips parted and a soft sigh escaped. From the pile of material, he drew a silk sash. He lightly ran the cloth down the valley between her breasts and in figure eights across her stomach. She pulled the cloth she was holding so tightly her knuckles turned white.

Sid circled her tits with the cool fabric, but never across her nipples. Sasha groaned as he once more stopped short of brushing against her pebbled tips. She arched her back, pushing her chest closer to him. Her breathing shallowed and came out in pants.

He chose a fabric with a harsher texture from the pile. Sid wasn't sure what it was, but he knew it contained wool. Instead of a light caress, he applied a bit of pressure as he drew the material over her sensitized skin. Goosebumps rose and her nipples hardened further. He took his time learning her every curve.

The sweet cooing sounds wreaked havoc with his cock. "I want to be inside you and I think you want me there."

"Yes."

"But you're not ready yet. You need to be much more aroused." That wasn't entirely the truth. He had little doubt he could bring her to orgasm, but he didn't want their play to end. Sid needed this time with her. Needed to build a bridge of trust and desire. He needed to prove to her that cuddling wasn't the only pleasure derived from sex.

"Jacob, I am. I really am. "

"It's a shame then that I'm in charge and I say differently." He knew his voice was smug and he didn't bother to hide it.

Her groan made him chuckle. She was so beautiful lying before him. As he ran the silk between her legs, she bucked her hips upward.

Sid drew the coarse fabric lightly over her clit. Her gasp sent his cock throbbing. Damn, she was perfect. He trailed his finger over the same path, pleased to find her as wet as he'd expected. Slowly, he slid his middle finger inside her channel. She was so tight she was going to strangle his dick. The mere thought of it shook his control.

Bending down, he pressed his lips to hers. She was intoxicating. As she opened for him, he plunged his tongue into her mouth. In time with his kiss, he thrust his finger inside her deliciously wet pussy. Her hips rocked forward to meet his assault. Over and over, his palm brushed against her clit.

As her body grew taut, he eased his touch, gentled and slowed his kiss. Pulling back was one of the hardest things he'd ever done, but he didn't want her first orgasm from him to be a cheap hand job.

As their lips parted, she groaned, her chest rising and falling rapidly. He stood and quickly removed his belt. After kicking off his shoes, he pulled a condom from his wallet then dropped his pants to the floor and stepped out of them.

"Don't worry, Sasha, I'm not going to leave you wanting." He slid the protection down his cock before kneeling at her entrance. "No second thoughts?"

"No, Jacob. I've never felt like this before," Sasha pleaded.

"We've barely gotten started, Misasha." He watched her expression closely as he slowly pushed into her. Her moan as they connected felt like sweet victory.

Sid kept his hands on her hips, holding her still. He refused to rush and hurt her.

For just a moment, he pushed everything aside and allowed himself to revel in the feel of her body. She was tight, unbelievably so, but nice and wet. Slowly, he moved a little deeper. Sasha was pushing against his grip, trying to force him in all the way. He chuckled as satisfaction filled him. Knowing she needed him as fiercely as he wanted her was a hell of a rush.

He was lost, no doubt about it. Her innocence touched him deep inside, bringing out his protective nature. If she was guilty of those heinous crimes it would tear his heart out.

This woman was different from the others he'd been with. He felt connected to her, drawn to be with her.

So many ideas were going through his mind, Dominant thoughts, dark and controlling. Would they send her further into a submissive space or dredge a memory from the past and ruin it for her? He didn't like playing in the dark.

"You're so responsive. Do you know what that means to a man like me?"

"No."

"It makes me harder than I thought possible. It makes me want to please you on a level you never knew existed." His voice was deeper than normal, more rough and primal.

She surged forward, burying his cock inside her. The air rushed from her lungs as he slammed home.

"Jacob, I can't take it." The lace at the corners of her eyes darkened as tears dotted the material.

"But you will. You've given me the power to decide and in return I will give you more pleasure than you've ever experienced before." Sid knew she was close and that she needed release. She needed to believe in him.

He drove into her over and over, making sure his strokes made contact with her clit. Her body tensed, her pelvis rose as she arched her back and pushed into him. Cries of pleasure bathed him in pride as her pussy contracted around his cock, sending him over the edge with her.

The force of his orgasm surprised him. With his focus almost solely on Sasha, he hadn't expected his climax to be so powerful. As he emptied himself into her, he felt more than a physical release. He felt like he'd come home.

Sasha struggled to bring her frantic heart under control. It had finally happened. She'd finally come during intercourse. She wanted to laugh or cry. Emotions were pouring over her at a rate she couldn't possibly sift through.

"Hold me, please." *Oh my, God.* How could she ask to be held, like some helpless child?

Jacob wrapped his arms around her and somehow struggled into a sitting position with her on his lap. He held her like she mattered to him. A sob was wrenched from her soul. She hadn't felt cared for in so fucking long.

Now that the dam had been breached she didn't know if she'd ever stop.

"It's okay, Sasha. I have you." His fingers tangled in her hair as he wiped at her tears.

His arms burned into her, locking them together. With him, in this way, she felt whole, as if she'd found a place where she belonged. She hadn't had that since her parents had died. Her brother had taken over her guardianship in name only. All he cared about was the money. He didn't seem to even grieve over their deaths.

She hadn't felt safe since. Until now.

It was stupid to feel such things from a virtual stranger. It had to be a post orgasm brain lapse or something.

"I'm sorry. I don't know why I'm crying. I get weepy when I'm tired, that must be it." She tried, half-heartedly, to put distance between them.

"Shh, relax." He rocked her back and forth. "Giving someone trust is difficult to do."

"Is that what I did?" She tried to tease him. "I think I tied your hands more than you tied mine." It took more effort than she'd expected to unclench her fingers from around the cloth he'd given her to hold.

Jacob helped her unwind it from her wrists. The ligature marks shocked her. She hadn't realized she had thrashed about so.

"As we experiment more, trust will come easier."

She found herself nodding even though it would never happen. How could it when she was going to have to run again?

"Talk to me, Sasha. Tell me why trust is so hard for you?" Jacob asked softly as he brushed her bangs away from her face.

Her entire existence was a lie. What could she possibly tell him? Tears burned the backs of her eyes and her throat threatened to close. She wanted so badly to make a life with him.

"Has a man hurt you?" Again his voice was gentle, coaxing her to answer.

She rubbed her cheek along his shoulder until she could find her voice. "Haven't we all been hurt at one time or another?" She didn't want his pity, and letting him in any further would just make the pain that much harder when she left.

"Point taken…" He ran his hand through his hair before meeting her gaze. "Once upon a time, I thought I was in love. She was a damsel in distress and I wanted to be her knight in shining armor." He gave her a self-deprecating chuckle. "Turned out she wasn't in need of rescuing. I was." He rested his forehead on hers for just a moment. "I trusted her to have my back. Instead, when I needed her most, she shot me. Literally." He lifted a patch of hair and showed her an ugly scar. "I know betrayal intimately."

Her heart ached for him. He'd shared a piece of himself and she felt the need to reciprocate. She wanted to tell him. It was on the tip of her tongue. The need to share her pain with someone who would understand was almost too great to ignore.

Sasha took several deep breaths and pushed away the hurt her brother continued to cause. Instead, she decided to share another horrific memory. This one was somewhat less heinous because it was perpetrated by a stranger and not a loved one.

"I had a meeting with a client. He lived downtown in an area that was part of a revitalization project. I had to park a few blocks away. By the time we were finished it was dark, the streets were empty. I was walking to my car when I was jumped from behind, beaten—" *Damn it*, her voice broke as the memories flooded her brain. "Raped."

Jacob held her tighter and rubbed his chin in her hair. "Did the police catch him?"

Going to the police wasn't an option. She couldn't have anyone looking too closely at her past. "No." Technically that wasn't a lie.

"Do you carry a gun or a Taser?"

She felt the tension running through him and wondered what was causing it. "I don't believe in violence."

"How about self-preservation?" He sounded terse, but his arms never relinquished their hold on her.

She had no answer for him.

"I don't understand that. If you'd been carrying a weapon then there would be one less bad guy out there." He kissed her on the temple. "Think of it this way, who would you rather have walking freely down the street, you or the bastard that did that to you?" His hand was rubbing her lower back.

She shook her head. "One person isn't more worthy than another." She couldn't take a life to save her own. She could never live with that. She shrugged. "He might change his ways, you just don't know."

"More likely, he will continue to rape until that loses its thrill and then he'll have to up the ante and perhaps starting killing."

"Or he could see the error of his ways, go to med school and find the cure for cancer. You just don't know." She refused to back down on this. "You of all people should be on my side. Look what a gun did to you."

"A gun is just an instrument. A batshit crazy woman I foolishly trusted did this to me. Besides, it's been my experience that people don't change. Not like that. If you've had better experience, please share because I just don't believe people can turn their life around like that." He slid her backward until their eyes met.

Sasha was stunned by the intensity of his gaze. Looking at him hurt. Tears threatened to streak down her cheeks again as she realized she wanted a chance with him. She didn't know if ride off into the sunset happy endings really existed, but she wished she could give it a shot with Jacob.

She looked away. Her life was a sham. She could no more begin a relationship with him than she could tell him her real name. Damn it. Why had she started this? If she just disappeared, as she needed to, Jacob would probably worry about her. That was the kind of man he was. Oh, she'd screwed up big time.

"No, I've never seen it happen, but I have hope it could." She vowed to be as honest with him as possible for the short time they had left together.

Jacob chuckled and kissed the top of her head. "Okay, my little pacifist, at least tell me you've taken ju-jitsu."

"Yes." She held a seventh level black belt. "I don't want to be hurt again…not like that."

A slow, sexy smile emerged from Jacob. He used his index finger and thumb to tip her chin upward, holding her in place when she desperately wanted to turn away.

Her face heated as fire streaked through her veins. Jacob looked like he knew exactly what she'd been thinking. His hand, splayed at the base of her spine, teased and taunted her. What would it feel like to be swatted? Would it be erotic or just hurt?

He cocked his head and seemed to examine her from all angles. She wished she could hide.

"Are you trying to tell me something?" His voice was an octave lower and glided over her skin like satin.

"I… No, I was just making an observation." Sasha realized this might be her one chance to find out what all the hoopla was about. While she couldn't come out and ask for him to spank her, she wouldn't turn it down either.

"Really? Forgive me, but I think the lady doth protest too much." His smile had taken on a definite smirk quality.

"I was discussing my reasons for learning martial arts." She gave him a sideways grin as she used her best haughty tone and tried to bluff her way through.

"So if I were to toss you over my lap and paddle your ass, you'd tell me to stop?" He slid his hand a little lower.

Where has all the air gone? She raised her eyebrow and tried to appear nonchalant. "What do you think?"

Jacob laughed. "I think you'd be startled, then as the heat spread and you grew wetter you'd want more."

She feared he might be right.

"Shall we find out?" The amusement had faded from his voice and an edge had taken its place.

God help her, she wanted to know. Where had her naughty streak come from? She never thought about sex, let alone kinky sex. Hell, she blushed when she read that kind of thing. Yet she couldn't deny her curiosity.

Shyly, she nodded.

"Say it, Sasha," he ordered.

Her heart began to pound and her brain grew cloudy. She licked her lips and sought her voice. "Yes." It was barely more than a whisper, but when his cock throbbed against her thigh she knew he'd heard her.

He wanted to spank her. What did that say about him? Was he just like all the other men she'd known? Was he excited by the idea of hurting her?

She began to tremble. What was she doing? Was she really that desperate for love?

His hand was applying pressure on her back, urging her into position.

"No. Don't." She tried to scramble off his lap. "I'm sorry, I've changed my mind."

"Whoa, Sasha. I told you before we began that nothing would happen that you didn't approve of ahead of time and I meant it. In return, I want your honesty. Why did you decide against it?" he asked patiently.

She shook her head. She couldn't talk about this.

Chapter Eight

"I know you're curious, so it isn't from a lack of desire. My best guess is you think it's wrong, that you can't quite wrap your mind around a spanking being an erotic pleasure. Am I off base?" He kissed her forehead, willing her to answer him.

She felt like heaven in his arms. She fit him. Her body melded perfectly against him. Jacob was slipping into the background and Sid was taking over. He'd considered coming clean more than once. He didn't want to lose her, and if his instincts were right, she was in serious danger. He needed to know the score, not to close a case, but to keep her safe.

He had to earn her trust and right now sex was the only tool available.

"Why do you want to hurt me? Why does that give you pleasure?" Her voice was thready and defensive.

"Hurting you would never bring me pleasure, Sasha. The very idea turns my stomach." There was so much more he wanted to say but he held his tongue, hoping she'd to talk to him.

"I felt your...you getting exciting about it." Her anguish rang clear.

"The idea of spanking you is arousing. Highly, in fact."

"See!" Sasha pushed against his chest.

Sid ignored her protest and continued his explanation. "Because you'll enjoy it. There is a bundle of nerve endings that can best be reached through impact. When done correctly, it can be very erotic. I won't say it isn't startling. The initial sensation is more sting than anything else, but rather quickly it evolves into a desirable heat. And frankly it's a naughty thrill for both of us."

She smiled but it didn't seem legit. He got the impression she wanted to believe him, but she was still struggling with something.

"Jacob" — she bit her bottom lip and looked up at him with tear filled eyes — "there are a lot of people in this world, both men and women, that get off hurting others."

"Yes, you're right. However, I'm not one of them." He debated just how graphic he should be. While Sasha may crave a caveman, she was still very skittish. "I enjoy rougher play than you might be used to." He took a handful of her hair and tugged. "A tingle along the scalp can get the blood pumping, can it not?"

She gasped and surprise registered across her face though she didn't move to stop him. Desire flared for a moment, her pupils dilated and her nipples peaked. Having made his point, he released her hair and massaged away the sting.

"Did I hurt you?" he asked, knowing the answer.

Sasha shrugged and turned away from him.

"No, you need to talk to me." He cupped his hand on the nape of her neck, ensuring she looked at him. "If you were to describe the sensation in one word would it be pain?"

"No." She answered quickly and with conviction.

He was making headway. "Did I harm you in any way?"

She chuckled. "Only my peace of mind."

He kissed her gently on the temple, knowing what that admission cost her.

"Now for the million dollar question. Would you want me to do it again?"

She groaned and tipped her head into his chest.

He clutched her hair again and pulled with constant, steady pressure that forced her head back so he could gaze into her eyes.

"Fine. Yes," she confessed reluctantly.

"Yes, what?" He refused to let her brush it away.

She glared back at him defiantly for a moment then she closed her eyes and took a deep breath before admitting the truth. "I liked it."

He released her hair and soothed away the ache. "Was that really that hard?"

"Yeah it was. I learned something about myself tonight and I'm not sure I'm happy about it. I guess I have a lot of thinking to do." She looked at the computer.

Oh no you don't, Sasha. You aren't getting rid of me that easy. "I don't want you brooding over this. Tell me what your concern is."

"You called me a pacifist and I am. There's too much violence in the world. I've always believed that, even as a kid. Now I've learned that I get all hot and bothered when you hurt me. That's wrong. I have defective genes or something. I don't want to be like that. Pain and pleasure should be on opposite sides of the continuum."

There was an easy way to show her the difference, but was it worth the price? "It's not violence and I didn't hurt you."

"It didn't tickle either, Jacob."

"It wasn't meant to. You are a strong woman and you want an equally strong man. There's nothing wrong with that. I didn't rip out your hair. You weren't harmed. It was a firm touch designed to focus your attention and quiet the rampant thoughts inside that head of yours. It was *not* intended to hurt you." Maybe if he said it enough times she'd allow it to sink in.

When she didn't respond, he tried a different tact. "Sasha, do you enjoy rollercoaster rides?" There were a lot of similarities he could draw from to help her see his point.

"I don't know. I've never ridden one."

Fuck. And he'd thought he led a narrow life.

"Sasha, can you honestly put an erotic spanking or rough sex in the same category as what that douchebag did to you?" He wasn't sure if he meant the rapist or whoever had set her up for the murder and arson charges.

"On the surface, no, of course not. But isn't the underlying need the same? Rape is about control. You said yourself, you like to be in control. You package it up with a romantic bow, but isn't it the same thing?"

Emotion surged through him. She was putting him in the same league as a rapist? He brushed the hair from his face, buying himself time to rein in his temper. He pushed her to talk this through with him. He couldn't very well jump down her throat for speaking her mind. "Have I done anything you've objected to?"

"Well, no," she admitted.

"Did I stop every time you asked me to?" It took determination to keep his voice calm when he was really seething inside.

Again she conceded, "Yes, you did."

"Then who was really in control, Sasha?"

She looked up at him, clearly confused.

"Would a rapist stop if you asked him to? Would someone who enjoyed causing you pain allow you to determine what activities you engage in? We're here alone. Physically, you're no match for me, Sasha. If my desire had been to hurt you, there would have been very little you could do to stop me." He held up his hand when she started to speak. "But instinctively you knew that was not my intent. No way in hell would you have put yourself in such a compromising situation had you had any fear of me. So what is this really about?" He waited while emotions flittered across her face. Surprise was the only one he was positive of.

"I wasn't accusing you of anything, Jacob. I realize now how it must have sounded and I apologize. In truth, I wasn't thinking about it from your perspective at all. You've been very patient with me, much more than I deserve. I don't question what type of man you are. I question what type of person I am. Have my life experiences warped my sense of love?" She flinched slightly then continued quickly. "Did the synapses in my brain get scrambled and now pain is pleasure and vice versa?"

"There's nothing wrong with you, Sasha. And patience should always be given freely." He hated bringing up the subject again, but it was the only way he knew to make her see the difference. "When the traumatic memories visit you at night, do you physically react?"

She snorted. "Yeah, I want to vomit."

He watched as his point hit home. "Giving control to someone you trust and having no control are two totally different things."

"Yes, you're right."

"But?"

She shrugged. "I just need to think about…things."

"Perhaps we should give you a few more things to contemplate." He was taking a risk. If she enjoyed it, as he hoped she would, it might confuse her further.

"What do you mean?"

He chuckled. There was no doubt in his mind that she knew exactly what he was talking about. "Over my lap."

The vein in her neck starting pumping double time. She bit her bottom lip and twisted her fingers into knots. He was a complete bastard, but he loved watching her. The more she struggled, the more aroused he became. She was going to choose him. He knew it. And knowing how hard that decision was for her made it all the sweeter.

"Now, Sasha." He spread his legs and set her on her feet between them. With one firm hand on her back, he helped position her. "Put your arms around my calf, remember to breathe and relax as much as you can."

His cock, hard and ready for action, was pressed against her hip. He didn't care. He had no intention of hiding his desire.

Her body was ramrod stiff. He had to give her time to get used to the idea. He rubbed her back, easing the tense muscles. "You're a beautiful soul, Sasha." Sid moved down her spine and caressed her cheeks. "There is nothing at all wrong with you. You have a healthy curiosity and we're going to do a little exploring."

He could feel her breathing quicken as his touch roughened. Sid used his forearm to keep her firmly in place. If she was in the zone, his strong hold would offer her a feeling of security and protection. After a few moments, she settled down.

As he drew his hand back, he felt her tighten up again. "Don't."

"I can't help it."

His hand landed hard on her ass. "Yes, you can."

Sasha squeaked, and if not for his forearm holding her down she would have bolted upright.

"You're fine. Nothing bad is going to happen to you." He swatted her other cheek then began to alternate back and forth. He gauged the strength of the impact on the sting and warmth of his palm. "If you reach a point where you can't take any more, all you have to say is stop."

She squirmed and bent her knees, lifting her feet slightly off the ground. "When does the feel good part kick in?"

Sid laughed. He couldn't help it. She was perfect. He'd given her ten swats before he rubbed all that glorious pink flesh.

Sasha moaned and arched her back. "Oh my."

His heart soared. At her obvious enjoyment, his cock jumped against her. He wanted to bury it deep inside her pussy. Finding the strength to wait was much harder than he'd anticipated.

He slid two fingers through her folds. "You're so wet." After a few strokes along her G-spot he pulled out and circled her clit.

"Jacob..." she cried as he stopped.

"Not yet, Sasha. I don't want there to be any doubt in your mind about whether or not you like this."

She groaned, but relaxed back across him.

He gave her five more then stopped and massaged away the sting. As the pain turned to pleasure, her fingernails digging into his calf began to relax. He doubted if she was even aware she was clawing him. "What are you thinking?"

"I'm not." She giggled.

The sound was more carefree than he could remember hearing from her. "What are you feeling?"

"Needy."

He plunged his fingers inside her pussy and curled them downward, stroking her where he knew she wanted it the most. With his thumb, he brought her clit to full attention. Her hips began bucking as he wound her tighter. The little sounds she made took his need to a new level.

She was beyond thinking, recrimination was out too. Maybe later, but right now she was living in the moment. This man, this stranger, seemed to know her body better than she did. How did that work?

Oh, God! She was so close. If he stopped again, she might not survive it.

"Are you willing to admit you're submissive?"

His voice held a laissez-faire tone that bothered her on some level, but it shouldn't have. She wanted him to stay impersonal, neutral, take it or leave it…didn't she? Friends with benefits, no strings attached was the only thing she had to offer.

"Only to you," she whispered, just before he took her over the edge.

Wave after wave of pleasure swamped her. The release was like nothing she'd ever experienced before. Her brain floated amongst the clouds as sensations overwhelmed her.

She felt his arms around her, holding her tightly as reality came back into focus. He kept telling her he'd keep her safe. If only he could. She choked back a sob.

Going there wouldn't solve a damn thing, but there was something she could give him.

His cock was pressed against her hip and she clenched her muscles, hoping he'd get the hint. With a growl, he took her to the floor and positioned her on all fours. She heard him rustling with something and wondered what he was waiting for. She wiggled her butt, hoping to entice him back to her.

"This is the last one I have with me. We need to make it count."

From her peripheral vision she saw a condom wrapper land on the ground beside them. A moment later, she felt him poised at her entrance. Leaning over her, he whispered, "You know...asses aren't the only thing that can enjoy an erotic spanking."

Before she could ask what he was talking about, his fingers began to drive her crazy, gliding over her clit in a circular motion. She found it hard to stay still as his cock slowly impaled her.

A satisfied sigh escaped her lips. She'd thought this position was too raw for her tastes, but she'd been wrong. He filled her completely and she loved it. She rocked back and forth in perfect rhythm with him. The pace was delicious, a slow and languid ride.

Suddenly his fingers swatted her clit. A shocked scream took the place of her sensual moans. She froze as he did it again and again, each time with slightly more force. Confusion filled her mind. She shouldn't like the sharp sting on her delicate private parts.

As his fingers swirled over her throbbing pussy, she thought she'd died and gone to heaven. "Oh, God."

Jacob laughed. "You're going to come for me like this and then you're going to thank me for spanking your pussy."

She had no answer for him. Her brain had disengaged, leaving her only capable of feeling.

He continued to pump into her as he swatted. Every few moments he'd massage the ache, driving her need higher.

She hung her head, panting, as every muscle in her body grew taut and ready to explode. Two more strikes and his silky command, "Come for me, baby," did the trick.

As she shook from her third orgasm, sensations flooded her system. They were now familiar but still bordered on too much to comprehend. From somewhere far away, she heard Jacob's guttural shout and knew he'd climaxed along with her. The constant noise in her brain, the never ending whirl of thoughts, was finally quiet as she collapsed, exhilarated and exhausted. Together they spooned on the soft carpet of her office.

* * * *

Sid woke with Sasha pillowed on his biceps. He hurt all over. Between the riding lessons, the fire and taking her like a man possessed on the floor of all places, his body was complaining, but his mind was at peace. It was more than just the fan-fucking-tastic sex too. He'd had great sex before, but it had never felt like this.

How was she going to take it when she found out he'd deceived her? He didn't want to deal with that until he had more time to cement her feelings for him. With some luck they'd track down Hackman quickly, and if he could keep her occupied at night, away from her storage unit, it might buy him some time.

He knew her first thoughts would be to run. He'd gotten too close last night. Her whispered comment,

'Only to you', told him she'd let him in, granted him something special. As skittish as she was, in the light of day that closeness was going to freak her out. He was going to have a bucking bronco on his hands once she woke up.

He noticed her breathing changed, but she continued to lie perfectly still, probably trying to find an excuse to send him on his way. *Sorry, baby, that ain't happening.*

"Hey, sleepyhead. Up and at 'em. If you're half as hungry as I am, then we need to hit a breakfast place ASAP." He bent forward and kissed her neck slowly, expressing with his lips what he didn't dare voice aloud.

Instantly the tension left her muscles and she tipped her head, giving him more access. His heart was tripping dangerously. He could not screw this up.

"I'm not a breakfast eater."

He clutched his chest and fell back onto the floor. "I'm crushed. Are you saying our evening was so uneventful you didn't even work up an appetite?" Sitting forward, he looked her square in the eye, daring her say the night had been anything but amazing. Personally, he couldn't remember ever clicking with a woman like he clicked with Sasha.

A beautiful blush stole over her cheeks. "I didn't say that." She looked around her office and began to pick up articles of clothing.

"I'm hungry, Sasha, and I don't want to eat alone. Besides, I need to take you back to your car anyway." He figured that would sway her and he was pleased when she nodded.

"Oh, I forgot. Okay. First dibs on the bathroom." She sent him a saucy smile as she dashed away.

While she was out of the room, he went to her computers, quickly duplicated all the files onto a flash drive, and installed a few programs that would monitor her keystrokes in the guise of firewall protection. When she came out of the restroom, he was standing naked behind her desk closing everything out.

Sasha stopped dead in her tracks. "That's a sight I never expected to see in my office. Rather pleasing though," she teased him.

He chuckled, glad to see she wasn't regretting her decision to be with him. "If I had more condoms, I'd bend you over the desk and eat my breakfast right here."

She blanched the slightest bit. "I think I need a shower before we consider anything like that." She swiped a hand through her hair.

"I believe you're perfectly edible as is, but it's a moot point because I know I wouldn't be able to stay out of you." He dressed in front of her, a little afraid that if he let her out of his sight she'd disappear on him. In no time at all, they were headed out to his car.

Sasha checked her watch and looked annoyed.

"What's wrong? Do you have an appointment this morning?" It would get really messy if she did. Protecting her in a situation like that would prove difficult. He took a thorough glance around the street as she locked the door behind them.

She shook her head. "My temp should have been here seven minutes ago." Her arctic tone spoke volumes.

The fact that Sasha didn't even use Cheryl's name didn't bode well. Most likely Cheryl was going to be looking for another job quicker than she'd expected. Sasha must be really irritated with her.

Sid walked Sasha to the passenger side, discreetly blocking her body from view as much as possible, and opened the door for her. Once she was safely seated, he went around to his side and got in. "Any preferences?"

Sasha had a sparkle in her eyes when she answered, "Surprise me."

They both laughed. Damn, it felt good, but it was short-lived.

As he pulled out into traffic, he noticed a car farther down the block enter the flow as well. It had been parked on the street and Sid thought it odd that he hadn't seen anyone entering the vehicle. It was possible the driver had been checking his phone or something else just as innocent. Then again, it could be Hackman.

He chose a family restaurant that he frequented occasionally. He was careful to always pay cash and never give his name. Plus, they had great food.

Using his rearview mirror, he kept tabs on the other car. It never got close enough that he could see the driver. Considering he was going at or below the speed limit, that aroused his suspicions as well.

"Ah shit. Don't tell anyone, but I made a wrong turn." He headed down an alley then snaked behind the bank. He stopped just short of the building's edge and waited.

"Is something wrong?" Sasha asked as she looked around.

"No. Not really. I was just trying to find another entrance. I don't want to look like an idiot by crossing four lanes of traffic just to turn back in one store later." He forced a chuckle.

Sasha tossed her head back and laughed. With her finger she drew an X across her heart. "Your secret is safe with me. If anyone tries to give you trouble, I'll say it was my mistake."

"Oh, no you won't. I take responsibility for my mistakes. It helps me learn not to make them again." The car should have driven by, but it hadn't. He couldn't stay there any longer without further arousing her suspicions. Slowly, he pulled forward. Even with the better vantage point, the car was nowhere in sight.

He pulled into the turning lane then almost immediately turned back. There were several other businesses on the street and the driver could have been headed to any of them. In his head, he tossed around the idea of going to another restaurant, but decided to risk it.

Over the years, he'd learned to listen to his gut instincts. They hadn't steered him wrong yet. Had he learned his lesson early on, he wouldn't have a slug inside his head. They'd been loud and clear that day and like a dumb-ass he'd ignored them.

Sid backed into a spot next to a retaining wall. If he needed to, he could make a quick getaway. He put his hand on Sasha's thigh. "Stay here. Let me get your door for you." He paused long enough to make sure she'd obey him.

Once they were out of the car, he set a brisk pace to the entrance. They were at their most vulnerable while out in the open. Sasha stayed right beside him. He scanned inside the café as much as the windows would allow before holding the door for her.

"Good morning. Good to see ya again," one of the waitresses shouted to him as she made her way to a table with an armload of plates and beverages. "Your spot's open." She nodded toward the back wall. "Earl Gray tea coming up. What can I get for you, sweetie?"

"Same thing, thank you," Sasha answered as Sid led her to his usual booth.

It afforded him a solid wall behind his back as well as a clear view of both the entrance and most of the kitchen.

"I see I'm not the only creature of habit," she teased him.

He shrugged. "If you find something you like, why goes elsewhere?"

Sasha looked at him long and hard. "You sound like you're speaking about something more important than where to eat."

Had he been? Probably. She was a very perceptive woman. Before he could answer, the front door swung open and a familiar face walked in. Suddenly the mysterious car made more sense. Instead of grabbing a booth nearby and watching their back as Sid had expected, Teague sauntered up their table.

"Hey, dude. You lose your phone? I've been trying to call you for hours." He grabbed a chair, swung it around backward and sat down like he owned the place. "Hi, I'm Teague. I work with Jake, when he sees fit to take my calls."

Sid's heart was pounding double time. For Teague to barge in, some bad shit had to have gone down. At least Teague had remembered his cover.

After grabbing his phone, he scrolled through his messages. There were about thirty of them, most weren't suitable for mixed company.

"Sorry. I must have had it on silent." This was awkward as hell. "I'll be in the office in an hour or so if you want to meet me there."

The waitress arrived with their teas and took their food order. To Sid's surprise, Teague ordered as well.

"No dice, brother." Teague picked up as if they hadn't been interrupted. "Someone trashed your apartment last night, stole your computers and took your lockbox. I think you know what that means." Teague scooted his chair slightly.

Sid noticed he'd effectively blocked Sasha inside the booth. Shit, that meant there was more and he wasn't going to like it.

"Oh, Jacob, I'm so sorry! Is this going to set you back at work?" She sounded genuinely distraught.

He brushed a hand through his hair as agitation swamped him. "I'm not worried about work, baby." Sid motioned for Teague to continue. He hated waiting for the other shoe to drop.

"Have you been listening to the radio this morning? There was a woman hurled off the 101 overpass this morning. She landed on a big rig." He grimaced. "Made a hell of a mess."

"Oh my God." Sasha's eyes kept glancing back and forth between Teague and Sid.

He reached across the table and held her hand.

Teague, Sid knew, was waiting on his approval. He'd already said too much to stop now. Sid motioned for him to continue.

"I believe she worked for you." Teague was watching her closely.

"Me? I only have one full-time employee..."

Sid saw the dawning cross her face. She must have remembered Cheryl hadn't shown up for work today.

"Are you a cop? How would you know all this?" The vein in Sasha's neck was pumping furiously. Without waiting for an answer, she tried to push past Teague. "I have to get back to the office. Please excuse me."

If he let her leave, he'd never see her again. Teague held his ground, as Sid had known he would. "Settle down, baby. No, we're not with the police. We can help you, if you'll trust me."

Immediately Sasha turned her attention to Sid. Her hand went to her throat and tears appeared in her eyes. "You played me."

"No, not like that, Sasha. Not like what you're thinking. Listen to me. In my spare time, I've been investigating a murder and arson case. A beautiful teenage girl, talented beyond all reason, was framed for the crime. I've been trying to find her. If my guess is correct, she's in grave danger and has been on the run most of her life."

"I have no idea what you're talking about. It's obvious you two need time to talk. I'll take a cab back to my car." She tried again to get past Teague.

Sid tightened his grip on her wrist. "I'm afraid I can't allow that...Alexa. It's too dangerous. If they've hacked my computer, they'll think I work for the FBI. There are files on there no one else should have access to. You have to trust me, baby. Take that leap of faith and let me help you."

She shook her head vigorously. "You're wrong. I don't know what you're talking about. Please, I need to get to the office." She tried to break free from his hold.

"Alexa, tell me what happened that night." He kept his tone calm, hoping to soothe her.

"My name is Sasha Powell. I'm an interior decorator. I don't know anything about apartments being broken into or girls dying on the freeways." Her voice cracked and she rapidly blinked. "You have me confused with someone else."

"Two nights ago I followed you to a storage unit." Shock and fury skittered across her face. "You slid underneath the door too quickly for me to see inside." He took a deep breath and admitted another lie. "I went back there yesterday. While I was there I found a dress form. Alexa Desman was a bright, upcoming clothing designer. I also found boxes of drawings along with a laptop. Before I could do a thorough search, a car pulled up outside. I hid in the shelving unit along the back wall. A major badass" — no, he couldn't sugar-coat it — "a mob-sanctioned killer named Hackman entered the unit. He found something of interest and left. As I was getting ready to leave, he came back and torched the place." He waved a hand in front of his face. "This is from the fire inside your storage unit, not a sunburn."

Her gaze flickered over his red, tender skin. "Oh my God, this can't be happening." She buried her head in her hands.

"Alexa, we can protect you. Tell me what happened," Sid urged.

"Was my laptop destroyed?" She looked at Sid as if the weight of the world rode on her shoulders.

The breath stilled in his lungs as her confirmation set in. There could be no going back now. The woman sitting in front of him was indeed Alexa Desman, wanted murder and arson suspect. And he'd spent the previous evening fucking her.

No, he couldn't distance himself like that. He'd made sweet, passionate love to her and he'd do it again the first chance he had.

"I downloaded all the files before Hackman came back."

She sat up a little straighter. "You did the same thing to my work computers too, didn't you? I even helped you do it." She shook her head and slumped into the seat, looking utterly dejected.

"Don't play the victim card, Alexa. You had an ulterior motive for asking me to look at your systems. I think you wanted my help." He refused to let her off easily.

Slowly, she raised her head and met his gaze.

He had no idea what was going through her mind and it scared the shit out of him. He was half convinced she was going to tell him to go to hell.

The waitress appeared, sparing him that agony for a few minutes. She distributed their food and left them alone.

Teague dug in, clearing his plate in no time. Both Sid and Alexa poked at their eggs more than they ate them.

"My real name is Sid Townsend. I work for the National Border Interdiction Agency. It's a law enforcement bureau that works under the radar to find and shut down, among other things, human trafficking rings." Sid felt Teague's gaze bore into him. He waved his hand, signaling Teague to back the fuck off. He was well aware he'd just breached a serious protocol and frankly, he didn't give a damn.

"When I search through the files from your laptop, what am I going to find?" He wanted her to tell him. It was selfish of him, really. He didn't want to break her confidence.

"Well, Officer, the files on my laptop were illegally obtained. Unless you had a search warrant, you had no legal rights to enter *my* storage unit, let alone break into *my* computer." A spark of indignation appeared in her eyes.

Teague smirked and Sid wanted desperately to punch that smug look right off his face.

"Ms. Desman, NBIA doesn't operate under the same constraints as the local PD. You won't find our agency on any government ORG chart. When we take you in and interrogate you on the charge of murder, arson, multiple counts of kidnapping and a plethora of charges involving the sex trade, we won't bother reading you your rights or giving you an attorney nor will one be present during our questioning. We play by a different set of rules," Teague announced, sounding quite pleased with himself.

"You aren't helping." Sid kicked Teague under the table.

"Yeah, well, my dick ain't clouding my judgment. What I see when I look at this cold fish is a murderess looking to find a technicality that keeps her from growing old inside a prison."

"Sir" — Alexa turned an arctic glare straight at Teague — "I've never much worried about growing old in prison or otherwise. I've been too preoccupied with staying alive to worry about some nebulous future."

"You notice, Sid, she's spouting a lot of righteous indignation, but she hasn't denied her guilt."

"What's the point? You're going to take me in whether I plead my innocence or not and once you do...I'm a dead woman. Jacob...Sid, whatever your name is, you seemed to have a fondness for animals. If that wasn't faked as well, please take care of Dakota for me. You'll find a stash of cash behind a fake wall in the closet at my apartment." Her voice was devoid of emotion, as if she was resigned to her fate.

Intellectually, Sid was pleased by her reaction, it was further proof she hadn't flown into a fit of rage and acted impulsively that fateful evening.

Emotionally, her despondency was killing him.

"Shut the hell up, Teague. Alexa, I'm not going to let anything happen to you. We're going to get through this." Whatever trust he'd earned last night, he'd obliterated this morning. Now, he was just one more asshole who had used her for his own gain. He needed to get her alone, to hold her and explain his actions.

Alexa spread her hand out on the table then looked up at him with a quiet loathing. "Those blisters on your fingers are from the reins." She lifted her hand and showed her calluses. "You're new to riding. That was part of the deception too." She tipped her head upward as tears pooled in her eyes.

Teague got his attention and nodded toward a white panel van waiting at the corner. Shit. Teague had called in the cavalry.

"Night night, princess," Teague whispered as he jammed the syringe into Alexa's thigh.

Sid lunged across the table, too late to stop him. "You motherfucker! Why did you do that?"

Teague had smoothly moved onto the bench beside Alexa and kept her from falling over. It irritated the hell out of Sid that Teague was cradling *his* woman.

"There's a whole restaurant full of witnesses, dumbass. Did you really think she was going to come along quietly?" Teague was completely unrepentant.

"Damn it, just damn it." Sid drew some cash out of his wallet and threw it on the table. "Give her to me."

"You're not going to do something stupid are you, Sid? The chief gave me orders to bring you and sunshine in, and in this instance, I gotta agree with him."

"Fuck you!" God, he wanted to take a swing or three at Teague.

"Dude, you're thinking with your little head right now. With the big guns in town, that shit just ain't gonna work," Teague cautioned him.

"You've been hanging around 'Bob' too long. He's got you talking like a moron." Sid knew Teague was trying to protect him, but that didn't make his interference any easier to accept.

"Maybe but, man, can he make an engine sing."

Sid drew Alexa into his arms, snuggling her close against his chest.

As they were leaving, the waitress stepped in front of them. "Is she okay?"

Sid leaned down and kissed Alexa on the forehead. "Hot tea. It gets her every time."

The waitress giggled. "Me too. See ya next time." She waved then went back to work.

Chapter Nine

She woke in a strange room with her head pillowed on Jacob...no, Sid's lap. Her mind felt fuzzy and her tongue too thick.

"I'm sorry, baby. I wish I could have told you the truth from the beginning, but you would have run. I know you would have." His voice was low and regretful.

Alexa desperately wanted to believe him.

"Last night...it was real, Alexa. I swear it wasn't a ruse. The connection we made was real. The only bullshit involved was the 'friends with benefits' ploy." His breathing sped up and his hand gripped her hair a little tighter. "I can't walk away from you. I'm in too deep. I hope there's a whole lot of Sasha in Alexa because I'm falling in love with her."

Hearing her real name roll off his lips made her heart trip dangerously, but when he uttered the 'L' word she panicked. When something sounded too good to be true, it was. "Do you always drug and kidnap the women you're in love with...Sid? Cuz, it seems a little counterproductive to the whole trust building thing."

God, help her. She wanted to believe him, but she wasn't ready to admit it or let him in on the secret.

"I can't really answer that. I've never been in love before." He fisted her hair near her scalp and gave it a sharp tug.

The sensation was familiar now. Strange as that was, she'd accepted it.

"You lied to me." She said it out loud to remind herself he wasn't the knight in shining armor he seemed to be.

"You lied to everyone," he answered simply.

He had a point. She could, of course, rationalize her reasons, but she supposed he could as well. "It hasn't done much good. My brother keeps finding me."

"Tell me about that night," he said softly.

There wasn't any reason to refuse. She felt no loyalty toward her brother and maybe, just maybe, Sid could help her stop him.

"How much do you know about my family?" she asked in a whisper. It had been her deepest, darkest secret for so long, shedding light on the truth was scary.

"You're Daniel Desman's daughter, heir apparent to the fashion throne."

She snorted then bit her lip trying to stem the tide of tears. Just the mention of her dad's name made her ache. She missed them so damn much.

"What happened, baby?" Sid urged her to tell him her story.

"My parents had died in a car accident a few months prior to Fashion Week. It was going to be my big premiere." She shook her head to clear out the fog. She still couldn't think about those days and not lose it.

"After their deaths, I couldn't complete anything. I couldn't focus. Danny, my brother, was so mad at me. At the last possible moment, he switched the line-up.

Danny pulled most of my designs and substituted Ezzy's, but he didn't give her credit. He wanted me to say they were mine."

She shifted so she could see Sid's face. "Ezzy saw the proposed press releases and was furious." She tilted her head in acknowledgment. "Rightfully so, too." Alexa drew her legs into a fetal position.

"Ezzy called me, thinking I'd stolen her work. I told her I didn't know anything about it and we agreed to meet at the studio and talk to Danny together. What he was doing wasn't right."

"How did he react when you confronted him?" Sid moved her bangs away from her eyes. "Was he trying to uphold tradition?"

"I don't think so. Everything was about money with him." She sighed and decided to share another painful memory. "Mom and Dad had taken care of every contingency. Years earlier, they'd bought burial plots for all of us, designed the services and prepaid for everything. A friend of theirs had been blindsided by an unexpected death and they didn't want us to have to go through the same thing." She sniffled and blinked, trying to keep the waterworks at bay.

"Danny cashed in the plots, canceled the services and had them cremated." It still hurt like hell that her parents hadn't received the burial they deserved. He fired tons of long-standing, loyal workers and hired...people with no experience. None at all." No matter how hard she'd argued, he'd refused to listen to her. Their parents' legacy was now in shambles.

"Let me guess, he hired girls, young, pretty girls," Sid guessed.

Alexa nodded.

"What happened when you arrived at the studio that night?" he asked again.

"It was late. No one was in the office area but Danny. He often stayed till the wee hours 'working'. Mostly he drank until the afterhours clubs opened then he'd stumble out of the office to go 'party'. When I got there, I noticed the lights were on in my office and Danny was inside. He was throwing my designs all over the place. It looked like a wind tunnel had exploded in there. I rushed in and that's when I saw her. Ezzy..." She broke into sobs.

Sid took her in his arms and rocked her. It felt so good to just be held. She took a few selfish minutes and soaked up his heat...and drenched his shirt with her tears.

He gave her a few tissues from the box on the coffee table and handed her a bottle of water.

She savored the cool liquid going down her throat. When she thought too much about that night it was like she was back there, reliving every horrible moment. After taking a few gulps, she knew she had to finish telling the rest or she'd never be able to.

"Ezzy had gotten there before me." Alexa could hardly tell it was her. He'd beaten her so badly. "She was on the ground between the desk and door. I think her neck was broken. The angle..."

She blew her nose and forced herself to continue. "I tried to run, but he was too fast. It felt like I was running in quicksand or something. He grabbed me and threw me farther into the office." The memories were choking her. She could still feel the blows and smell the smoke.

"Did he hurt you?" Sid asked gently.

She closed her eyes and tried to come back to the present. She nodded and took another swallow of water. "He must have thought he'd killed me too. He took a hammer to my computer then poured gas all over."

In her mind's eye, she watched as he tossed her handspun fabrics into the mess. "He threw a match and the room just exploded in flames. As he ran out the door, he tripped over Ezzy." Alexa shuddered. "He'd wedged her body in the doorway and I had to move her to escape." She looked at her hands, remembering how cold Ezzy had felt and how searing the flames had been. "I should have gotten her out of there. I read she'd been burned almost beyond recognition. For a while, they'd thought she was me."

"Your brother encouraged that theory. It would have given him access to your trust fund," Sid explained. "What did you do next?"

"I was so freaked out. I had no illusions that my brother was a nice guy, but I hadn't thought he was capable of murder. When I saw a police officer on the street I thought the nightmare was over. I begged him to make sure everyone was out. Instead he threw me into the back seat and drove me to the warehouse district. He parked down some alley. I almost convinced myself I'd entered *The Twilight Zone*. Sometimes, I don't think I ever left it."

"Which warehouse? Was it one of yours?" Sid sounded intrigued.

She shook her head. "I was so scared. I had no idea where I was or what to do, but my fight or flight instinct was in full swing. When he came to the back door to open it, I kicked out with both feet as hard as I could. He hit the building and I took off running. I heard him yelling behind me, but I didn't slow down until I was several blocks over. Eventually I went up a fire escape and sat on the roof of a building. Once the sun came up, I planned how to get out of town."

"Are you sure it was a cop?"

Great, she'd probably just offended the only possible ally she had. "He was in uniform and driving a cop car." *Okay, that came out pretty damn snarky.*

"What's on the laptop?" Sid changed directions with his questioning, throwing her off guard.

"Not enough. Just copies of emails and screencaps from social media sites, messages, that sort of thing. He's pretty brazen, especially on Twitter."

"How do you have access to his emails or messages?" Sid's voice had taken a softer tone again.

"He hasn't changed his password, or not significantly, in all these years. I've found several accounts that I *know* are his." She watched him carefully as she let go of another secret. "Once I tried sending the information anonymously to the FBI. If they'd acted on it, they could have saved twenty-one women. He calls them bolts, like bolts of fabric. Since all the manufacturing is now done overseas and bought in significantly larger quantities than that, it wasn't hard to figure out. But instead of stopping him, they showed up on my doorstep, searched my apartment and I was back on the run again."

Her head was pounding and her arm, under the cast, was itching, small inconveniences in the big picture, but just one more reminder of her current predicament. She had no idea where her purse was, and if she found it chances were Sid wouldn't allow her to root around inside it for Advil. No matter how good his arms felt, he was still some sort of cop and she was still his prisoner.

"Was it Cheryl Teague was talking about?" She wished her voice had sounded stronger. Appearing weak was rarely beneficial.

"I'm afraid so. We still don't know if she was working with them or just collateral damage."

She snorted. "Yesterday I would have said collateral damage but then you found her computer password-protected. I don't know what to think now."

Alexa moved off Sid's lap and sat at the far end of the couch. Taking comfort from his touch seemed like a foolish habit to get into. "So what happens now?" she asked softly.

"I'm going to get you some Advil," Sid told her, before standing and walking to the door.

She looked at him sharply.

"You keep rubbing your temples. I figured you have a headache. I'm also going to talk to my boss and get us the hell out of here."

* * * *

Sid pulled up outside Alexa's apartment with Sammy and Teague in tow. It pissed him off to have babysitters, regardless of the fact that they were his two best friends. The chief hadn't been amused with his disregard for policy. He was lucky to have walked out of there with his badge and gun in place and Alexa on his arm.

"Stay here. We'll only be a few minutes," Sid told his friends.

Alexa had shied away from Teague and remained silent since they'd gotten into the black NBIA Suburban.

As Sid held the door for Alexa, Teague added his two cents. "Yeah, I know your idea of a 'few minutes'. Don't take all day, man. We're supposed to meet up with the detective handling the toss job on your place in less than a half an hour."

Sid flipped him off as he and Alexa went up the stairs to her apartment. "Are you doing okay?"

Alexa nodded as she searched in her purse he'd returned to her.

"Are *we* okay?" he asked softer, slightly surprised he'd voiced his real concern.

She faltered on the steps and shot him a quick glance before answering. "You can drop the pretense, Sid. I'll tell you whatever you want to know."

"I'll tell you what I know... You didn't kill anyone, Alexa. The murders were a crime of opportunity and rage. It doesn't fit your personality at all. Your brother had a good attorney and he used your disappearance to muddy the investigation, but his luck is about to turn." Sid carefully considered how to phrase his thoughts. "Alexa, I've got your back. You're not alone anymore. We're going to see this through together."

One quick nod was the only response he received, and frankly her silence was killing him. He'd never felt like he had so much to lose.

He took the keys she pulled out of her handbag and opened the door for her. After a quick look inside, he was relieved to see everything was neat and orderly. Apparently Hackman hadn't uncovered her address yet. Probably because Cheryl hadn't known it to give him. It was only a matter of time though. "Grab your get away bag. You won't be back here for a while," he ordered after they'd entered the apartment.

Without saying a word, she went to the closet, shoved a wood panel out of the way and removed a duffel bag. She carried it into bathroom, unzipping it as she went.

Sid watched her kick the door closed then heard another one open. He assumed it was a linen closet because he had the only exits in sight.

Alexa gasped and something dropped to the floor.

Instinctively, Sid pulled his Sig Sauer from his shoulder holster. "Alexa?" he shouted. His heart rate doubled when she didn't respond.

A moment later, the door swung wide and Hackman nudged Alexa into the room. He had a gun shoved against her temple and his arm across her chest, locking her beside him.

Son of a bitch. He should have checked the apartment before he let her out of his sight. Damn it. "You don't want to do this." Sid tried to reason with Hackman.

"I don't want a problem with you, Townsend. Do as I say and we'll all walk out of here in one piece," Hackman told him.

That he knew Sid's name didn't bode well. That Sammy and Teague were parked right outside was their ace in the hole. If Sid could stall long enough they'd have help. "Let her go."

"Not happening. *This* girl is pure gold. You're not just another sorry-ass bolt are ya, honey? I learned that from the files on your desk." Hackman snickered. "Did you know your boyfriend here is a cop who plans to arrest you for murder?"

"Sounds better than what you have planned for me," Alexa shot back.

"Life sucks, honey. Get used to it. So, Townsend, since you clued me in to her true value, I'm feeling generous. If you put down your weapon and kick it to me, I'll let you live. What's it going to be?"

Sid knew Teague and Sammy would be watching the door and would respond as soon as Hackman left the apartment. "Just don't hurt her." Sid bent down and slid his pistol straight toward Alexa.

As soon as Sid's fingers released the grip, Hackman turned his weapon on Sid.

Alexa screamed, "No," and tried to pull Hackman's arm away. The bullet's impact spun Sid around. He couldn't breathe, and it felt like his chest was on fire. He crashed into Alexa's coffee table, tipping it over as he hit the ground.

He forced air through his aching lungs and reached for his second pistol tucked into the small of his back. As he scrambled to face Hackman, he heard three shots ring out and a body hit the floor.

Oh God! He turned, expecting the worst, but instead Alexa sat on the ground with Sid's Sig Sauer in her hands. Hackman had a hole in his throat and was slumped against the wall bleeding out.

Just as he reached Alexa, Teague and Sammy came through the door with guns drawn. "Check out the rest of the apartment, make sure it's clear," Sid ordered, afraid of any more surprises.

Alexa sat staring at Hackman. Her hands were shaking so badly, Sid was afraid she'd hurt herself. "It's okay, baby," he whispered as he carefully pried her fingers from his weapon. He pulled her into his arms, turning her away from the gruesome sight. "Thank you, Alexa. You saved my life."

"We're clear," Teague yelled out.

Sammy caught Sid's attention. He motioned that Hackman was dead and that he was going call it in.

"I couldn't let him kill you." She began to sob. "You did what he asked and he still tried to shoot you."

"He *did* shoot me." Sid pulled back and showed her the hole in his shirt and the marred area on his vest.

Alexa's eyes grew wide and her hand covered her mouth as she whispered, "Oh my God."

"It hit the vest, baby. I'm okay." He smiled. "If you hadn't reacted, he would have killed me." *Or kept trying anyway.* He wanted to ease her conscience if possible.

Blood from Hackman was seeping across the tile nearly to Alexa's shoes. She drew her legs back and tried to scramble away. Sid picked her up instead and carried her past the body. The apartment was so small there was no place he could take her to shield her from the sight.

"The local PD is going to be here any minute. We need to get her someplace safe. Finish packing, Alexa." He urged her into the bathroom to finish getting her things as he made the phone call to his boss.

Once he'd reported in, he returned to her.

"Sammy, the old man is going to text you with an address to a safe house. Get her there ASAP." Sid turned to Alexa and cradled her head in his hands. "Go with Sammy, baby. I promise he'll keep you safe. I'll be there just as soon as I can."

"I want to stay with you," she pleaded with tears in her eyes.

"The local cops can't know you were here, baby. They'd ask too many questions we just can't afford to answer right now. Trust me, please. Sammy's a good guy. He'll keep you safe." He waited impatiently, knowing every second counted now.

From the doorway, Sammy took a good look at the stairwell and surrounding area before he motioned Alexa to follow him out.

"Alexa?" Sid stopped her. "Promise me you'll stay with Sammy until I can get there."

She gave him a quick nod then started to leave.

"No, say it out loud." He was suddenly panicked that if he let her leave now, he'd never see her again.

"I promise, Sid."

Chapter Ten

Alexa sat huddled in the back of the large SUV as Sammy drove her to the safe house.

"Was that the first time you've ever had to kill someone?" Sammy asked, ending the silence.

"Yeah." She didn't want to talk about it. Talking about it made it real.

"Hackman was a straight-up killer, Alexa. He knew Sid was in law enforcement. To someone like Hackman, that meant Sid had to die. Only one of them was walking out of that apartment. Personally, I'm glad it was Sid." Sammy kept watching her in the rearview mirror.

"How long have you worked with Sid?" Alexa had to change the subject before she started crying again.

"We were in the Marines together, did our graduate studies at Quantico, received our yellow bricks together too. But that's not what you really wanted to know, so stop hedging and just ask," Sammy urged her.

No it wasn't, but even that little bit of information hit her hard. Sid had a master's degree and she hadn't even finished high school. The differences between them were greater than she'd thought. A few years back she'd bought forged papers so she could take some college courses, but that was a far cry from graduate school.

Sammy seemed willing to talk and she decided to take advantage of it. "Sid used a cover story when we met. I don't blame him. I wasn't upfront with him either, but I don't know how much of it was real and how much of it was a lie." Somewhere along the line, she'd fallen for Jacob. It was stupid considering how little she actually knew about the man. She hadn't meant for it to happen, but there was no denying the way she felt.

"You want to know if he was playing ya?" Sammy glanced back at her. "That's not Sid's style. He's always been a little too by the book for that. If he told you he cares for you, he means it."

"I'm pretty sure he took riding lessons and rented a horse to arrange our first chance meeting," Alexa pointed out as they circled the same residential block for the second time.

"Actually, it was my rig. I can't tell ya how much fun it was to teach him how to ride. I honestly worried he wouldn't be able to walk the next day." Sammy laughed. "He was determined to make a good show of it."

Sammy turned down an alley and parked the SUV. "Look, Alexa, I need to hop that fence and get the keys. I really don't think you're up for that." He sighed as if he wasn't pleased with his options. "I'm going to lock the doors. If you take off, the alarm will blare and I'll have to chase your ass down. I'm not in the mood so do me a favor and just sit tight."

"I'm not going anywhere. I'm tired of running," she answered honestly.

Sammy took the keys and locked the doors before jumping over the fence.

Alexa knew she should run. Odds were good she'd end up in jail when all this was through. She got the impression from Teague he'd like to personally lock her up and throw away the key.

It didn't matter. She didn't have the energy to outrun her past any longer. She was exhausted both mentally and physically. Alexa leaned back in the seat and closed her eyes. *Foolish.* All she could see was Hackman and that huge gun of his pointed straight at her face. She shivered. She'd been so afraid of what Sid would do. Her death didn't matter. In some ways, it would've been a relief, but she knew Sid wouldn't allow that to happen without a fight.

She couldn't live if Sid were injured or killed because of her. Danny, her brother, was never going to stop searching for her. She had no idea why he hated her so much. A couple of years back he'd had her declared dead, granting him full access to her trust fund. She'd hoped he'd leave her in peace, but that hadn't happened.

Alexa jumped as the locks unlatched and Sammy took the driver's seat. He didn't say a word as they slowly left the alley and pulled onto the street. Nearing the third house on the block, Sammy aimed a clicker out of the window. He then pulled the SUV into the garage, closed the door again and exited the vehicle.

After finding Hackman hidden in her apartment, she was a little hesitant to walk into a strange house. That fear galled her. She'd let it run her life for so long now. She grabbed her satchel and followed him in through the kitchen entrance.

"Stay here. I'm going to check the rest of the house," Sammy ordered.

As she waited, she wondered, if she managed to evade jail, would she still be forever on the run, always looking over her shoulder? What kind of life was that?

"All clear," Sammy yelled from the back of the house.

She didn't know what that meant, but there wasn't any sense of panic in his voice so she assumed everything was fine and took a seat on the couch.

When Sammy came back into the room, he took a seat opposite her. For a few awkward moments, she sat staring at her hands while she felt Sammy's eyes scrutinizing every inch of her.

"Say what's on your mind," she demanded, unable to take the silence any more.

"Sid's going to take the fight to your brother's doorstep. Where do your loyalties lie, Alexa?"

Surprised by his question, she lifted her chin and met his gaze. "Not with Danny, if that's what you're afraid of." She didn't trust the NBIA though either. Teague didn't seem to care that she was innocent. He seemed more concerned with closing a case than finding justice. As far as she could tell, he figured she was wanted for murder, therefore, she was guilty of murder. If only life were that black and white.

"That wasn't the answer I wanted to hear," Sammy told her solemnly.

"What do you want from me?" She refused to lie just to make him feel better.

"Sid and I have been through a lot together. I'll always have his back whether he thinks he needs it or not." He continued to stare at her without even blinking.

If she'd had something to hide, his behavior would have unnerved her. "I'm glad. He's a good guy. And if he's going after my brother, I hope he has a loyal army at his back."

"Do you love him or is he just a convenience?" Sammy asked, pulling no punches.

She snorted in the most unladylike fashion. "None of this has been convenient." Alexa had no intention of discussing her feelings with anyone except, possibly, Sid. It didn't feel right to share those details with someone else.

"You didn't answer my question," Sammy pointed out.

"That's between me and Sid. I've only known him a short time and most of that was full of lies and cover stories."

"I don't know if Sid ever mentioned it or not, but I'm part Native American. My people believe in soulmates. Listen to your heart, Alexa. It knows the truth."

That was the first time Sammy had mentioned his heritage. "Not to be flippant, but how would I know what the truth is? I've never felt real love before. Betrayal is the only thing I've ever found. Considering all the lies between us, it doesn't seem like Sid is any different."

"Don't let your head or logic get in the way. Love is never logical, but if your instincts aren't telling you Sid is the one, then don't play around with him." Sammy grew very solemn. "You don't want me for an enemy, Alexa, and if you harm Sid, I'll be your worst nightmare."

She already had enough of those. "I would never knowingly hurt Sid."

"Do you have any idea what he's doing right now?"

Alexa sat up a little straighter. There was an edge to Sammy's voice she hadn't heard before. "What do you mean? I assume he's telling the police what happened and doing paperwork."

"He's falsifying reports, lying to the cops and covering your ass at the possible expense of all our careers."

"What?" She jumped to her feet.

"He's telling them he shot Hackman," Sammy explained.

"He can't do that. Call him, tell him to stop." Alexa didn't want Sid getting in trouble for her. When Sammy made no move to call him, she grabbed her satchel and headed for the door. "Fine. I'll turn myself in."

Before she reached the knob, Sammy blocked her path. "You're either sincere or one hell of an actress." He took her by the arm and led her back to the couch. "Relax. He'll be here soon."

She slumped against the cushions and breathed a sigh of relief. "You lied, just to see what I would do."

"Actually, I told the truth, just to see what you would do." He threw her words back at her.

"Then stop him." She sat forward as the desire to wrestle his phone away from him became almost too strong to suppress. "I don't want him to take the blame for me."

"It was a good shoot. Did you forget Sid was hit first?"

"So why lie? Just tell them I did it," she pleaded with him.

"Think it through, Alexa. If Sid allowed that, your name would be all over the police reports and the danger to you would increase tenfold," he explained patiently.

Sid was putting himself and his friends in a terrible position to protect her. A lump formed in her throat and tears filled her eyes. She didn't want anyone taking a risk for her, especially Sid, but it warmed her as nothing else could.

"What can I do?" She needed to give back, to do something for him in return.

"Don't betray him."

* * * *

Sid was anxious to see Alexa, but he owed Sammy the curtesy of bringing him up to speed. "The local PD didn't question much. I think the cover story will hold."

"I never knew you had such bad aim. I guess the stress was just too much," Sammy teased him.

Sid flipped him his middle finger. He'd already endured enough ribbing from the locals. "I doubt she's ever handled a gun before. I'm certainly not going to be pissed that it took her three shots to get the job done. The only thing that matters is she did it."

Sammy held up his hands. "You'll get no argument there. She's one tough lady. You're a very lucky man. I'll stand guard. You go be with her. She's had a rough day."

Sid found Alexa in bed. He wasn't sure what had transpired between her and Sammy, but she'd won his friend's support. He breathed a small sigh of relief over that one.

He sat on the edge of the mattress and marveled at the woman who had fast become more important to him than he'd believed possible in so short a period of time. Tears stained her cheeks and she sniffled every few seconds. She'd obviously cried herself to sleep. He watched her for a few moments as he stripped off his pants and shirt then lay down beside her.

Alexa's eyes fluttered and she started striking out. He tossed his leg over her thighs and clamped her wrists in his hands, protecting them both. "Alexa, wake up, baby. You're safe now. I've got you." Sid was concerned that if she kept thrashing about, she'd reinjure her wrist.

Once her gaze locked with his, she relaxed. She trusted him whether she realized it or not. He released her immediately.

"I'm sorry. I was dreaming..." she whispered as she buried her face in his chest.

"Looked more like a nightmare from this side of the bed." He ran his fingers through her hair and held her tight. It had been a long ass day and he just wanted to lose himself in her.

"Help me forget, Sid."

"How?" He knew what she needed, but he wondered if she was willing to admit it.

"Make love to me," she answered with her head bowed.

Sid tipped her chin upward. "Anything else?"

Her face flushed. "Dominate me."

"My pleasure, baby." He was honored she'd turned to him. Her independent streak was too highly developed for her to lean on others often. That she turned to him meant a great deal.

"Tell me what you want, Alexa." Being what she needed was his top priority.

Her eyes widened and she tried to turn away. Sid held her by the chin, refusing to let her hide. For a moment they were in a silent battle of wills, their gazes locked, neither ready to give any ground.

"I don't know," she answered softly.

That he understood. "Fair enough." It wasn't always easy to put feelings into words. He decided to offer her choices. "Do you want to be restrained?"

She froze for a moment while searching his face for something. Reassurance? A second or two later, Alexa shrugged.

"Use your words, baby. That action can mean different things to different people." He also wanted her comfortable sharing her innermost thoughts with him. The only way to achieve that was to talk. A lot.

"Like before...where I can get free if I need to." She was timid in her response, as if unsure of how he'd react.

Sid wondered how long it would take before she freely spoke her mind. "Impact?" he asked, watching her closely.

A shy smile danced across her face. "Yes."

"Yes, please," he corrected.

Alexa repeated the phrase as pink dusted her cheeks.

"Good girl." He decided to press his luck. "Pain?"

She flinched and closed her eyes as if reluctant to answer. "Maybe the tiniest little bit."

"I'm proud of you, Alexa, I know that wasn't easy to admit. Thank you." He kissed her forehead. "I can work with that." He altered his tone, made it slightly more commanding. "Get undressed for me."

As she carried out his order, he grabbed his gym bag he'd dropped by the door as he'd come in. He set several condoms on the nightstand then pulled out an eye cover.

Alexa followed his directive then sat on the bed with her knees pulled up. She gripped the sheets, but only drew them over her feet.

He handed her the black satin sleep mask. "Put this on." He had to bite his tongue not to add 'please'. Manners were ingrained in him, but Alexa didn't need a nice guy right now. She needed him to take charge. "Lay down on your back, arms over your head, legs apart."

Once she complied, he gathered a few other implements and put them within reach.

She was so beautiful, he had to dig deep to maintain control. His cock was already hard and ready to take her. He didn't doubt her innocence any longer. Now he only had to figure out how to remove the threats to her so they could build a future together.

He slipped his belt under her forearms and pulled it through the buckle without latching it. "Lift up your head."

She followed his instructions immediately, allowing him to slide the tail under her. Alexa would have no way of knowing whether he'd honored her request unless she tugged on it. He was curious to see whether she would. In a small way, it was a test to see how much faith she had in him.

Now that her sight was blocked, he set a few more implements within easy reach.

"You saved my life. Thank you." Sid ran his hand along her cheek.

Alexa cringed. "I took a life." She looked sad and shaken. "You did what he asked. You put down your gun, but it didn't matter. He was going to kill you regardless. I just couldn't let that happen."

"Why?" Sid had little doubt that Alexa would have allowed Hackman to harm her, yet she'd gone against her principles to save him.

"You're a good man. And… And I care about you," she answered softly, hesitantly.

"I'm falling in love with you," Sid confessed.

Alexa turned her head in his direction and her complexion lost several shades of color in an instant. He chuckled knowing the blindfold was hampering her view.

"Don't freak out on me, baby. You're very loveable. It was bound to happen." He tried to keep it light, hoping that would allow her to remain calm.

"It's not safe." She shook her head in agitation. "Even if I avoid jail, I'm still on the run. That horrible man wasn't the first one to come looking for me. I've started over so many times."

"Shh, baby. It's okay. I've got a plan that I'll tell you about later. Right now, we're going to get your mind off this unpleasant business." He drew his hand between her breasts.

Her lips parted and a soft moan urged him on. Sid continued down to her pussy. He lightly teased his fingers over her lips and down her thigh. Though her senses seemed heightened, her muscles were relaxed. Her trust in him was growing quickly. Now was the time to keep the momentum going. "Tonight, if you need me to stop I want you to say the word 'red'. Do you understand?

"Red?" she asked quizzically.

"That's right, babe. Say the word 'red' and I'll stop immediately."

"Okay, but why can't I just say stop like before?"

He appreciated that she was willing to question him. "Sometimes, as our play intensifies you might feel like you *should* say stop without really wanting our session to end. Does that make sense?"

"Not even a little bit." She smiled, teasing him. "I'll take your word for it and keep 'red' on my tongue's speed dial."

"Good plan." Sid took his Wartenburg wheel and followed the same path his fingers had just traveled.

Her lips parted and he half expected her to call out her safeword, but she cooed instead.

As he neared her clit, she clenched her jaw shut and drew her legs closer together.

"Open." His tone was firm and unrelenting.

She whimpered but went back to her previous position.

"Good girl. Have a little faith and give this a try. If you don't like it or it becomes too intense, you know what to do."

Her breathing had quickened and her hands balled into fists, but she nodded.

Slowly, he continued. The only pressure he was applying was that of the wheel itself yet the sensation, he knew, was potent. He was exceedingly careful, making sure the spines stayed on her labia only. After she relaxed a little, he'd explore her limits.

Once he'd completed the path, he traced another. This time in ever tightening circles leading to her nipples.

"Oh! Sid...I'm scared." Her voice quivered the slightest bit.

"And it's exhilarating, isn't it? You're getting wet and your need is growing." He spoke with confidence.

"Yes," she answered begrudgingly. Her knuckles were turning white as she strained to stay still.

Sid was diligent, always keeping the teeth of the wheel moving freely, never allowing them to bind and truly hurt her.

With the circuit completed, Alexa breathed a sigh of relief.

"You love it. You know you do."

She tipped her head sideways as if considering his statement.

Sid gave the side of her breast a subtle whack with a crop.

A surprised shriek sent him laughing. "You shouldn't keep your Dom waiting for an answer, subbie. I want immediate, honest responses, not ones you think I want to hear."

"Okay."

He gave her a series of strikes with the flexible leather square before he returned to using the wheel. This time he rolled those sharp points directly over her nipple.

Alexa bit her lip, moaned and pushed her torso deeper into the mattress, away from him.

"I would advise against moving around." He was pretty sure his arrogant, amused tone was setting her teeth on edge, but also helping her to sink further into a submissive mindset.

"I can't help it," she complained.

If they'd been together longer, he would have offered to tie her down, but she wasn't ready for that. "Continue squirming and I'll stop."

She pushed out her bottom lip in a cute as hell pout. "You're being mean."

Sid swung the crop direct onto her pussy.

Alexa's fingers flared out as if reaching for something and she yelped again.

"I am not mean." He told her with infinite patience. "I'm giving you exactly what you need." To emphasize his point, he dipped his index and middle finger into her channel. "Aren't I?"

She shook her head. "I want you inside me."

He set aside the crop and continued his leisurely stroll across her body with the wheel. "That's a desire not a need. You *need* me to take you on a journey, to explore your senses and show you what your body is capable of. There's a big difference."

"I'm on fire, Sid." Her breath was coming in pants and her coos were growing louder with each touch.

"Let me stoke those flames even hotter, baby." As he bent forward and took her taut peak into his mouth, he shimmied out of his briefs. She was so expressive she had his body begging for mercy.

With an urgent need to be inside her, he pulled away long enough to slide a condom over his cock. Before he climbed on the bed and between her legs, he grabbed one more toy. Good thing she was wearing a sleeping mask because his grin was likely evil.

Sid nuzzled her breasts, licked and flicked the nipples until she was arching her back off the bed. "This is going to pinch, baby. Tell me when you've had enough." He slid the clamp around her rosy peak and began to tighten it.

Alexa was biting her bottom lip again and her hands were balled into fists. His heart clenched as she squirmed and he willed her to say the word. This was as much an exercise in building trust as it was a moment of pleasure. He needed to trust her to communicate with him in these matters.

"Stop. No more." She drew her elbows closer to her breasts.

He knew she'd waited too long and backed it off slightly. This wasn't a test of her endurance or a punishment. When she gave him a short sigh of relief, he knew he'd been right.

To distract her and to give himself a modicum of relief, he gently pushed his cock inside her. Her worried expression vanished and desire took its place. After a stroke or two, she matched his rhythm. A few more and he stopped.

Her groan of annoyance put a grin on his face. "You're lopsided, baby, we have to fix that."

"No, no we don't. I don't mind," she replied quickly.

Sid took a moment to read her body language. A pretty pink blush covered her cheeks. She could have been embarrassed for speaking up or she could be shy because she liked the bite of pain and her mind was playing games with her again. He glanced at her hands as he continued to look for clues to the truth. When he saw Alexa's fingers were relaxed, not curled into a ball, he decided to continue.

"You know how to stop me," he reminded her as he forged ahead.

His earlier statement rang loudly in her ears. '*You might feel like you* should *say stop without really wanting to.*' That was exactly it. She felt she should make a token effort to avoid adding another ache to her overly sensitized body, but she'd be disappointed if he didn't continue.

Her mind was swirling. Though she tried to get a handle on her emotions and logically process what was happening, it was impossible. Nothing made much sense anymore. Being scared was exciting, she craved it. Somehow Sid walked the line between enough pain to heighten her arousal, but not so much that it turned her cold.

This time as he tightened the clamp, she spoke up sooner. She'd learned the 'too much' threshold happened quickly. "Stop."

Part of her was surprised he listened and she felt a twinge of guilt for doubting him. She hadn't trusted anyone in so long it seemed a foreign concept.

"That's my girl." He laid the chain in the valley between her boobs.

The cold metal almost took her breath away. Even the slightest brush of his skin against hers felt electric, like her nerves were hyper aware.

Sid's long, sure fingers gripped her waist as he began to thrust deep inside her. Each forward stroke jiggled her throbbing nipples, sending fire straight to her pussy. It was too much. Panic started to rise.

"I've got you, Alexa. Relax, baby, and let it happen." He tipped his pelvis forward, connecting with her clit.

Every muscle was clenched tight as she fought the inevitable. It was too much. If she came now, she feared what would happen. The feelings were too intense, she'd lost control.

He slowed his pace. "You belong to me, Alexa, and I'm going to take care of you. We're a team, together in all things. Give yourself to me."

His words were killing her. She wanted everything he was offering and she wanted to be there for him, to give him the moon and stars in return. "Sid!" She screamed his name, a plea for him to catch her as she let go.

Her orgasm tore through her, a tornado of sensations and emotions. She rode each wave, amazed at their strength. As the force began to ebb, Sid removed the nipple clamps. Fire raced along her veins. Sid's hoarse cry as his orgasm hit was the last thing she noticed before the world faded away and pleasure took over once more. For a time she simply floated in a sea of white noise, her mind at peace as her body hummed with delicious aftershocks.

Slowly she became aware of Sid cradling her against him. He was nuzzling her hair and whispering softly. She never wanted this moment to end. She feared it was a dream, but it seemed too perfect to even be that. Her nightly adventures into dreamland resembled horror film more than a romantic naughty girl flick.

"I'm not going to let you escape me." His hot breath bathed her neck, causing chills down her spine.

"Is this how you subdue all your prisoners?" She was definitely putty in his hands.

He tickled her ribs until she was begging him to stop.

"You know that's not what I meant." He held her until she settled again. "I can say in all honesty, I've never apprehended a felon while my pants were off."

She laughed. Sid was fun to be with. How had he become so important to her so quickly? Her parents had met, fallen in love and married within two months. When retelling the story of their whirlwind engagement, her mom would often say after the first date she just knew he was the one.

Could Alexa get as lucky? It didn't seem possible.

Chapter Eleven

Sid sat at the kitchen table eating breakfast with the three people who meant the most to him and sincerely wished two of them weren't there.

Alexa hadn't said a word since she'd sat down with them. Her back was rigid and she rarely lifted her eyes from her plate, though she had eaten next to nothing.

It was easy to see Teague's and Sammy's presences made Alexa uncomfortable. He kept glancing her way, wishing she'd meet his gaze. He should have spoken to her alone, but it was too late for that now.

"We acquired Hackman's cell phone." Sid needed to lay out his plan and see if she was willing to help. Keeping it from her was starting to bother him. He didn't want secrets and what felt like a sin of omission between them. He would demand full disclosure from her and he planned to honor her with the same.

"Oh?" Alexa stopped picking at her food, instantly alert and on guard.

"Based on the texts, we know Hackman was hired by 'Desi'. We're assuming that's your brother. We've kept his death under wraps and we're continuing to message Desi with daily updates. Desi instructed Hackman to deliver the 'bolt' to the usual storage facility."

Alexa laid her fork on the plate and sat up straighter in her chair.

"Did you know Hackman?" He was pretty sure what her answer would be, but he needed to ask.

"No, he must have met Danny after…" She looked at her food, anywhere really but at him.

"And yes, Desi is Danny." She answered as if resigned to her fate. "That's been his nickname since high school. I guess it goes without saying that I'm the bolt."

"Hackman was an enforcer for the trafficking ring we suspect your brother is affiliated with." Sid kept the conversation moving in hopes she wouldn't focus too much on the past.

She nodded though she was clearly lost in thought. "What happens when Hackman doesn't show up?" she asked quietly.

"Don't worry your pretty little head about that," Teague interjected.

Alexa ignored him and continued to look at Sid expectantly. It warmed his heart that she focused completely on him, effectively shutting out anyone else.

He winked at her and smiled. She immediately blushed and looked down at her hands. "We're working on it. The problem is, we don't have any direct evidence pointing to Desman's guilt. He's a small time player and the agencies that we know are investigating the ring haven't focused any real attention on him. They have enough to bargain with. Both the DEA and FBI are interested in flipping him, but they don't see any value in arresting him. At this point, it would only jeopardize their investigation."

"Flipping him?" Her eyes bored into Sid.

He wished he had something more to give her. "Using him to testify against others more culpable."

"He killed Ezzy and he gets a free pass?" She pushed her breakfast plate into the center of the table and leaned away from everyone.

"We need evidence. It's his word against yours," Teague informed her.

"And he has the cops on his side. So I'm screwed." She leaned back against her chair and closed her eyes for a moment.

"No, Alexa. We're going to bring him to justice, but right now we lack enough evidence to take it to court," Sid explained as gently as possible. He scooted closer to her and rested his arm on the back of her chair while he ran his fingers along her neck.

She met his gaze and tapped her finger against the table. "How? If he doesn't see Hackman at the meeting place, he's not going to stick around. He isn't stupid."

"We have reason to believe the drop isn't a face-to-face meet. The 'bolts' are left drugged and restrained in a storage container. Once delivered, Desi transfers an agreed upon sum into Hackman's account in the guise of a 'consultant fee'," Sammy explained. "When he goes to the drop, he's only expecting to find you."

The blood drained from Alexa's face as she pushed her chair away from the table. "No, no way." She hurried down the hall to the room they were using.

"Good job, man, now she hates us both." Teague patted Sammy on the back as Sid followed Alexa.

He reached the door as she slammed it closed. He blocked it from hitting him in the face as she ran inside the bedroom. "Come here," he ordered.

Her steps faltered, but she continued her path. At the entrance to the bathroom she turned and looked at him. It was only the length of the room separating them, but the emotional cavern was growing ever wider. "Come here," he said again, softer this time.

Alexa tipped her head to the side and exhaled. "Sid..."

He spread his arms and remained silent.

"You can't boss me around." She leaned on the door frame and bowed her head submissively.

"Come to me. I need you." His tone was more of an enticement than a command.

She pushed off the wall. With shoulders slumped and her gaze on his feet, she closed the distance between them.

Alexa stopped a foot or so in front of him.

He gladly met her the rest of the way and engulfed her in his arms. "Thank you, baby."

"I can't do it. I can't serve myself up like a sacrificial lamb. Don't ask me to, Sid. You don't understand what he's like." She grabbed his lapels and buried her face against his chest.

"I love you, Alexa. Do you really think I would put you in a situation where you would be harmed?" He understood her reticence, they were just building a semblance of trust, but he didn't like it.

"I won't let anyone drug me, Sid. Not even you. Not even under a doctor's care. I have to have my full faculties. I can't be caught unaware."

She couldn't possibly know what she was doing to him. He could feel her trembling. The urge to secrete her away was almost more than he could ignore. "I wouldn't expect it of you," he assured her.

"Teague did it before and I suspect he'd have no qualms with doing it again," she snapped in a fit of temper.

"It will not happen again. You have my word on that. Besides, he won't be accompanying us to New York. He'll be of more help to us here." As he felt a bit of tension ease from her tight muscles, he hid his smile in her beautiful hair. Teague was going to have a hard time extricating himself from the mess he'd made this time. Alexa may be a pacifist, but she clearly held a grudge. "I'm not making excuses for him. He was way out of line, but he thought he was protecting me."

"And next time his excuse will be 'it was for the good of the investigation'. Men like that always think the end justifies the means." She glared at him defiantly.

"I'm running the case and I will not allow you to be harmed," Sid repeated, hoping it would sink in. "I won't lie, baby. We need your help to nail him. And I have no doubt that facing him will be difficult, but seeing him brought to justice will go a long way toward easing your nightmares and it will get you your life back. No more running. You can buy some land and start your own horse rescue if that's what you want."

She stepped away and turned her back toward him. "I could have done that with Jacob, but I don't know if Sid even likes horses."

His heart stuttered for a moment. She was including him in her future plans. Sure, she was saddling around the subject, but she was thinking of them together after this mess was cleared up. A terrible weight lifted off his shoulders. He went to her, wrapped his arms around her shoulders and kissed the top her head. "Sid loves you and if horses make you happy then Sid likes horses just fine. I don't have much experience with them. Sammy gave me a crash course, emphasis on the crash, but I want to learn more. They're spectacular animals, protective and smart. I can easily see why you fight for them."

She leaned her head against his chest. "I don't know you and you're asking me to put my life in your hands."

"You know I'll keep you safe, Alexa. You can believe that." Sid waited, knowing she had more on her mind.

"You confuse me." She sighed. "On an almost instinctive level, I do trust you and it scares the hell out of me. There's nothing logical about it."

"I feel the same way. I would hand you my gun and never think twice about it. I know you would do anything in your power to keep me safe. You've already proven it. In that moment, you could have shot both me and Hackman. My back was turned to you and there were plenty of bullets. You had your get away money and the exit out the back was clear. You could have started over, just like you've done so many times in the past. Instead, you saved me and stuck around knowing there are murder charges still hanging over your head. You wouldn't have done that if you didn't trust me." Nothing else mattered.

Slowly she nodded. Their eyes locked and he felt as if he was seeing into her soul. He knew they were meant to be together.

He sat down on the bed and took her hands in his. "Alexa, you own my heart. It's a little war-torn and beat up, but it's all yours."

Tears dotted her lashes and she blinked rapidly. "You're killing me, Sid. You're handing me everything I've ever wanted on a silver platter. I've been alone since I was just a kid. I never imagined I'd find a man to spend my life with let alone have the opportunity to settle in one place. I've never dreamed of a house or a ranch of my own. It's not that I didn't want it. I just try to be practical, set goals I have a prayer of achieving." She looked up at him expectantly. "Do we have a chance at making this work? Really?"

He wasn't sure if she meant a successful relationship with him or bringing Desman to justice. It didn't matter, he planned to make both happen. "Absolutely. I won't let you down, Alexa." He took her in his arms and held her tight.

"I'm afraid," she confessed.

"I'll keep you safe."

* * * *

Alexa sat in the back of Hackman's van as they drove through the warehouse district down by the docks. NBIA had 'secured' Hackman's New York apartment and storage unit. There were so many holes in this plan it was too scary to contemplate. Chances were good Danny wouldn't stop to visit. He'd probably come in guns blazing and all her worries would be over. She hadn't voiced her concerns because she was afraid Sid would stop her from going through with it. As the days had gone by while they'd traveled across the country and prepared for the showdown, she'd realized just how right Sid had been. She needed to see this through and she needed to be an active participant.

As they'd made their way from Phoenix to New York, Sammy had explained what they knew about Danny's role in the human trafficking ring. It killed her to know their family business was being used as a front for a sex slave ring. Her heart went out to the young men and women who were brought here under the guise of legitimate employment opportunities only to find themselves drugged and chained inside a dark steel jail at the mercy of someone like her brother.

She had allowed fear to rule her life for too long. It was time to stand up to Danny and see that he paid for what he'd done, not only to Ezzy, but to every other living soul he'd reduced to a 'bolt'. Their lives mattered and it was time he was held accountable.

"Coming up on the unit. Keep your head down," the driver ordered.

A microphone had been woven into the waistband of her pants and another into her braid. The handcuffs she wore had a hidden release catch and a short dagger was concealed in the heel of her shoe. None of which would do her any good if Danny decided to shoot first and chit-chat later.

She had every confidence though that if he did kill her, he'd rot in jail for at least that crime. She'd take some solace in that.

"Remember, Alexa, you're supposed to be drugged," Sid reminded her. "We haven't spotted Desman yet, but that doesn't mean he isn't here watching. We're on his home turf now. You're doing great, baby. We have you in sight and the unit is wired for both sound and visual. I'm not far away. At the first sign of trouble, you say the word and we'll be there."

Buried into her right ear canal was a bud allowing her to hear Sid. His calm reassurance was keeping her anxiety at a manageable level. Sid had no idea how hard it had been for her to get into the van. While it made perfect sense to have an agent that resembled Hackman drive the vehicle, it had been damn near impossible for her to stand calmly while they handcuffed and placed her inside with a stranger.

"Don't come rushing in until you have the evidence you need to convict him. I'll be fine." Danny had always been a hothead with a quick temper. Chances were good he'd smack her around a bit as she goaded him into incriminating himself. She knew Sid's first response would be to rush to her rescue and she needed to head him off before he ruined their only chance. "I can take whatever he dishes out, Sid. You just make sure to get it all on tape."

"We're here." The driver kept his head down and pulled the brim of his baseball hat a little lower. "Just like we practiced, Alexa. Stay limp. You're supposed to be barely conscious. Do me a favor though, don't hit my spine with that cast of yours. I'd rather not be paralyzed."

Alexa forced a chuckle since he was trying to keep things light. Shame it didn't help much. She still jumped as the back door swung open. As the agent tossed her over his shoulder in a fireman's carry, she managed to relax her taut muscles and ignore his collarbone biting into her ribs with each jarring step.

The storage unit was nothing more than a shipping container like the ones she'd seen on flat cars in trains or stacked high on cargo ships. It smelled of urine and sweat, causing her stomach to roll. For a moment, she allowed her imagination to consider what the other 'bolts' had to have felt as they'd ended up in this wretched place. Terror soaked through to her bones.

"Breathe, Alexa. I'm here, baby. It's going to be okay," Sid whispered through her earpiece. "Stay focused."

The NBIA agent posing as Hackman dropped her on a dirt covered, crusty brown square of carpet and clipped the chain of the handcuffs to the rigid steel walls of the unit. "Good luck, honey."

Though she was trembling with fear and nearing panic, she was still determined to see it through. Danny needed to be stopped.

She watched as the driver slid the door open far enough to slip out. Light reflected off several hooks attached to the walls. How many 'bolts' did they normally bring at one time? Would being with others help or make it worse? Watching someone be battered would tear Alexa apart. She'd rather be hurt herself than watch another suffer.

As the door slammed shut, panic engulfed her. It was so dark she couldn't see anything around her. Little scratching noises had the hair on the back of her neck rising. She imagined all manner of bugs crawling toward her. A shiver sent the chain jangling. It was crazy how loud things sounded in the dark. How long would she have to wait? Her shoulders were tingling and her arms were going numb from being held above her head. She shifted around, but it was impossible to get comfortable. Would she be able to get the handcuffs off if she needed to? She supposed when her life was in danger she could muster the strength.

"I asked a realtor friend of mine to look for horse property in the north valley. There's a couple of places near where you ride that I want you to see. Do you want to buy land and design the facility yourself or buy something already set-up?" Sid whispered to her.

His voice took her mind off the stench and her aching muscles, allowing her breathing and heart rate to settle.

"I don't care about the house. Something simple and utilitarian works fine for me. I have some ideas about the barn and tack room though." She'd lived in hovels for so long it didn't matter, but having the opportunity to help abused and neglected animals meant the world to her.

Over the last few days, she'd realized that Sid needed a balance in his life almost as badly as she did. In his work, he saw all the horrors one human could do to another.

"A van has circled the area and is slowly approaching the unit, Alexa." Sid was all business now. "What's your code word, baby?"

"Parents," she answered immediately. They had wanted a word that wouldn't raise his suspicions, one that would feasibly fit into a conversation, but still alert the team to trouble.

This was it, if everything went according to the plan, Danny would be arrested and she would be free to start her life over.

"He's out of the vehicle and heading straight for the unit. We're moving in, Alexa. Just keep him talking," Sid advised her.

"Don't rush it, Sid. Let's see this through," she whispered as the door rattled and slid open.

The beam of a flashlight hit her dead in the face, blinding her. Though her heart was hammering in her chest and thumping loudly in her ears, she focused on the man shuffling toward her. Something was off. Unless her brother had changed dramatically, he'd sent someone else. As he drew near, the smell of sweat and dirt were overpowering. Her brother had always poured on the cologne. No way was he Danny.

"So what has the Hatchet left me this time?" the man muttered as he tipped her chin upward.

"Where's Danny? That man that brought me here said" — she shrank away from the stranger — "he said, he was taking me to my brother, Danny, Danny Desman." She kept her voice small.

The man froze. "Brother? What the fuck? Desi don't have no sister that I ever heard of."

"I'm so confused." She hung her head down. "I know if I could just see Danny we could figure this out. He's my big brother. He'll tell you this is all a mistake."

"Those drugs are making you loopy, sweet face. Desi would fuck over his own mamma, but you'll see him soon enough." He held up a syringe in front of the light. "You gonna give me any trouble?"

"No, please, I just want to see my brother." The light continued to bob in front of her eyes so she couldn't get a good look at him, but he didn't sound like anyone she'd known from her childhood.

The handcuffs drew tighter as he unclipped the hook holding them over her head. Her hands swung down into her lap. The blood rushing into her shoulders and arms brought the feeling back and with it pain.

"Step into this," he ordered, holding out a sailor's style duffel bag.

"I want to see this through," she answered softly, hoping to keep Sid and his men from rushing to her rescue. Alexa knew this was their one shot at catching Danny.

The man snickered. "That's good, sweet face, cuz you're gonna. But 'Danny' ain't gonna save ya. He's gonna sell ya, and knowin' that bastard, he'll train ya himself. I could see him doin' his own sister. He's a crazy fucker."

A shiver went down her spine. She'd been warned the transmitter wasn't very strong. Once she drove away with this man, she would probably be out of contact and on her own.

"No, you'll see. He loves me. This is a mistake." If he believed she'd go with him quietly, maybe he wouldn't drug her.

"You're one dumb bitch, ain't ya? I bet Desi gives us all a free ride. He gets off hearing the dumb ones scream and fight."

The punch to her abdomen came out of nowhere. Air rushed from her lungs and she doubled over in pain.

"What happened, Alexa? Are you all right?" Sid shouted through her earpiece. She tipped her head away from the man, hoping he couldn't hear.

"I won't try anything. Please don't hurt me," she managed to get out through gritted teeth.

"Just warming you up, sweet face. Get used to it. Sometimes pain is the only way to know you're still alive." He chuckled then hefted the bag, with her curled inside, to his shoulder and began walking.

He turned sideways and used the momentum of her body to bounce the door farther open. The air rushed from her lungs and pain crashed along her ribcage. Somehow, she kept from groaning. A few more steps and he dropped the duffel bag. She landed on her back and rolled sideways to stop her head from hitting the road. To keep Sid from freaking out, she took the abuse as stoically as possible.

A moment later, she was hurled through the air. She brought her hands up as far as she could and tucked her head down. As she hit the side of what she assumed was a van, part of the cast on her wrist shattered. Her sharp scream of shock and pain allowed plaster particles into her mouth and down her throat. Tears streamed down her face as she coughed uncontrollably. Her stomach muscles, already tender from his punch, knotted and cramped, making it almost impossible to catch her breath.

"Alexa, baby, talk to me," Sid whispered through her earbud.

She tried to respond, but all she could do was cough.

"Baby, are you all right?" Sid asked again, this time with an edge of desperation.

By the time she had control again, the man was settling into the driver's seat and she dared not speak.

As soon as he started the vehicle, music blared from the speakers. He dumped the clutch and pulled away. Each time he changed gears, Alexa struggled to stay in one place. There was no doubt in her mind he was doing it on purpose.

"I'm okay," she said softly, hoping Sid could hear her.

"We're" — static crackled — "you."

"You're breaking up, Sid. If you can hear me, don't worry. I'm fine." Okay, so that was a lie of the highest order. She hurt like hell, but she wasn't in immediate need of rescuing, at least not yet.

The canvas of the duffel bag was scratchy and stiff. Each time the vehicle stopped or turned, Alexa strained against it, scraping her knees and elbows into a raw mess. She focused on plucking away the rest of her cast. It was good to have something to occupy her mind besides fear.

"Fuck," the man shouted and turned the music down. "If you make one sound, I'll make your death long and painful. You hear me?"

"I won't, I swear," she answered as meekly as possible as she caught the faint sound of sirens. *Oh Sid, what have you done?*

Alexa felt the van slow and pull over to the side of the road.

"Shut off the ignition and show me your license, registration and proof of insurance card, please."

The steady vibration of the motor ended abruptly as she lay perfectly still and prayed Sid hadn't called a stop to the operation.

Some clunking sounds, she assumed was the glove box lid opened and slammed shut, filled the silence. It was impossible to see anything clearly but a beam of light illuminated the area near her.

"What do you have in the back?" the officer asked.

"My tools and drop clothes and shit. I'm a painter," the man answered in a perturbed voice.

"Where are you headed this evening, Mr. Grumer?"

"I'm en route to meet a client and I'm late, so if you're going to give me a ticket, can you get on with it?" he grumbled.

"You were doing forty-two in a thirty-five. Slow it down, Mr. Grumer, or next time I'll write you a ticket," the officer warned.

"No problem," Grumer replied, then started the van.

Once they were back on the road, Grumer shouted over the radio, "Maybe I won't turn you over to Desi. Maybe I'll keep you for myself, sweet face. I think you're my good luck charm."

"We've got a GPS transponder on the van and a transmitter boosting your signal, Alexa. Talk to me. I need to hear your voice, baby." Sid sounded calm, but she knew he was stressed.

"I'm okay. I feel better knowing you can find me. I love you, Sid, and I do trust you." She needed to say it, just in case.

"Hell of a time to tell me, baby." He sounded strained, but amused.

She suddenly remembered everyone could hear her. Only Sid's comments could be directed solely to her. "Sorry, folks, for the TMI, but sometimes you have to seize the moment," she apologized.

Alexa was pretty sure the agents with Sid would give him a hard time for her indiscretion and the thought made her smile. Funny how even in the midst of a dangerous situation, with just about every part of her body hurting, Sid could still make her smile.

"No worries, baby. You can tell me you love me any time." He was definitely laughing now.

Sid was one street over tracking the van Alexa was riding in. He wished to God he could trade places with her. Acting as support was always trying. Boring as hell for ninety percent of the mission, but that ten percent when your friends and colleagues were in the line of fire he'd always considered as the worst part of the job. Until this. Having Alexa in danger as he rode safely behind her was pure hell. He knew first-hand just how quickly a case could go to shit and this one had already gone awry. Of course, they had planned for every contingency, but Sid had expected Desman to go to the unit himself.

Something was off. Alexa had been the only witness to Ezzy's murder, with Alexa dead he'd be home free. So if he planned to kill Alexa, it stood to reason he'd want to limit the number of people who could link her back to him. Yet he wanted her alive. Why?

"Alexa, you mentioned that Desman had you declared dead. When was that?" He hadn't run across the official paperwork and he should have.

"A couple years ago. I hacked into his computer and saw his correspondence with an outside lawyer." Alexa was breathing heavily.

Adrenaline could do that, but he suspected she was in pain. The urge to pull her out of there was almost too much to ignore. "Outside?"

The agent that had pulled over Mr. Grumer had reported seeing five gallon paint buckets, a small compressor and other painting accoutrements. Every time Grumer hit a bump or turned, Alexa was likely getting banged around in the back of the van.

"Desman's Designs has used the same lawyer, Mr. Hawkings, since my parents founded the company. He was emailing someone from a different firm." Alexa groaned softly. "I don't remember the name right now. I saved copies of all their correspondence on my laptop."

"I have the files. I'll look for it." Sid would have known if a request had been filed. He'd definitely have to look into the attorney as well.

"Do you...?" Static.

"Alexa?" Knots tightened in his gut. "Alexa?" He picked up his two-way radio. "I've lost contact. What's going on?"

"The van turned into an underground parking garage. We've sent agents in on foot," Sammy answered from one of the other surveillance vehicles.

What the fuck?

Chapter Twelve

"Sid? Can you still hear me?" Alexa asked for the fourth or fifth time. *He's been quiet too long. Something's happened. Did Grumer figure it out and lose them? Oh God.*

The vehicle had been stopped for a minute or so, but was still running. Were they waiting for a train? Oh no. What if Grumer put her back in a storage unit and packed her away on a train? Sid would never find her.

Metal clanked then she was dragged about two feet. Someone grabbed her by the hair and pulled her head through the top of the duffle bag.

"You're no fun, sweet face. I like to hear crying and begging," Grumer complained, right before he shoved a syringe into the side of her neck and the world grew fuzzy.

The van had been out of range for approximately five minutes. Five long fucking minutes. When it reappeared on GPS, the sounds being picked up from Alexa's mike were completely different, the road noise was considerably louder, the music was gone and she wasn't responding. Calling the end to a mission was a serious decision, but Sid made it instantaneously and without any reservations. It didn't matter that he was probably blowing their only chance to bring in Desman. Alexa's safety was more important.

Sid gave the order. "Intercept the van. We're pulling Alexa outta there."

"You got it, boss," Sammy immediately responded through the two-way radio.

Sid's driver cut across a parking lot and pulled the city water department truck they were using to the curb a block away from the suspect's van. Grumer was out of the vehicle with his hands on the hood, yet the road noise from Alexa's mike was as loud as before. "Fuck! She's not in the van. He moved her to another vehicle."

"Are you sure? The officer is still searching the back," Sammy asked cautiously.

"Her signal is growing weaker. She's in motion," he answered as alarm spread like fire. "Get us moving before we lose her completely," Sid ordered his driver.

"What direction?" the agent driving the water department truck asked Sid.

"Back toward the garage." If he were Desman, he'd have sent Grumer in the opposite direction. By pulling him over again, they'd shown their hand. If Desman was keeping track of Grumer, he'd know Alexa was baiting him. "Detain Grumer until further word from me."

"We'll transport him to the safe house. Good hunting, Sid. I'll get what I can from him and relay it ASAP," Sammy informed him.

Sid feared he would need it. As they backtracked to the garage, Alexa's signal grew faint. He reached out to every agent involved in the investigation. "What other vehicles were seen leaving the garage once Grumer entered?"

The list the undercover officers were rattling off was terrifyingly long. Sid linked his laptop with the Transit Authority's network and began to track the vehicles using traffic cameras, as well as bridge and toll pass stations.

While they were following Grumer, Alexa's signal had started to fade, so Sid focused his officers in the other three directions, hoping to reacquire her signal.

Fear clawed away at him. Was Desi one paranoid SOB or had they somehow tipped him off?

As Sid coordinated the search, he hung on to the hope that Desi needed her alive. Hackman's orders had been to retrieve her, not kill her.

* * * *

Alexa awoke with a start. Her vision was fuzzy and she couldn't move her arms. Flashes of light drew her attention. Was it storming? She heard whimpering and crying, but she couldn't see where it was coming from. Each time she tried to pull her hands down she heard metal clanking and something bit into her wrists, sending excruciating pain through her arm.

More flashes had her blinking and looking around. A man's voice, patronizing and cruel, sounded off to her left.

"Cry harder, honey. You're turning me on." Flash, flash, flash.

A shadow crossed over Alexa's face and she instinctively tried to pull away. The bright flash of a camera hit her eyes, blinding her momentarily.

"Nice tits on this one. Older though."

Alexa looked down. *Dear God,* she was naked. She tried to cover herself, but her hands were secured over her head. Failing that, she drew her knees up to her chin. From where she lay, she could see two rows of cots. Each row had four women, like her, handcuffed and stripped of all clothing. Her heart sank. They were in a large, fairly dark room. Two men, one in faded blue jeans and the other in camo, were walking around taking pictures of the women and chatting nonchalantly with a third man that Alexa couldn't see.

Once each woman had been photographed, the men left. With the immediate danger past, Alexa took stock of her situation. It wasn't good. When they'd taken her clothing, they'd also taken her only source of communication with Sid and the dagger she'd had hidden in the heel of her shoe.

Unless Sid had somehow followed them, she was on her own.

The girl closest to her was huddled in the fetal position, softly crying.

"My name's Alexa. What's yours?" she asked quietly.

The girl hesitated a moment then sniffled. "Crissy."

"Do you have any idea how we ended up in here?" If she could learn how they abducted the women, maybe they could figure out how to protect others before they ended up in a place like this. *That's assuming, of course, that I get out of here alive.*

Crissy's chin trembled as she shook her head. "It was supposed to be a photo shoot. My big chance."

"It'll be all right, Crissy. We'll get out of here…somehow." Alexa prayed she wasn't lying to the girl.

"This one?" the man wearing jeans asked, as he walked toward Crissy. He had tats along both arms and a carefree smile.

"Yeah, the scrawny blonde. She's the next Sophia Vergara, don't ya know?" a man answered from behind Alexa.

The guy in jeans blocked Alexa's view, but she caught glimpses of Crissy struggling so hard she was rocking the cot.

"She ain't no Sunny Leone, that's for sure. No damn tits. Settle down, Sophie, you'll be feeling right fine in a few minutes." He started laughing as he walked back out of sight.

"Alexa?" Crissy whispered.

"I'm here," Alexa tried to reassure her.

"I feel funny. I'm all tingly and hot. What did they do to me?"

Alexa's gut twisted and she renewed her attempts to get free. Each time she tugged the pain in her wrist sent bile to her throat. "I don't know, Crissy. Try to stay calm."

"My crotch is on fire, Alexa. Help me," Crissy pleaded as she rocked her hips back and forth.

"Breathe deep, Crissy and stay calm. It'll pass." Alexa knew she was lying. Whatever they'd done to the girl wasn't going to go away quickly or easily. Damn it. She had to get loose.

Alexa remembered the handcuffs had a special release clasp. If she could just reach it, maybe she could do something to help the girl.

Suddenly the other half of the room was flooded with light. It looked like the inside of a cheap motel. A bed, curtains, dresser and lamp were visible. If she could get free, she might be able to break the window and get out.

To reach the catch on the handcuffs, she had to slide them farther down her arm. Either they had tightened or her wrists were swollen because she couldn't move them enough. The skin was abraded and the cuffs hurt like hell. Her left arm, where the cast had been, was pale and bruised.

Mr. Faded Jeans made his way back to Crissy.

"Leave her alone!" Alexa warned.

He turned and looked at Alexa as if she were gum on the sole of his shoe. "You don't talk to me like that, bitch." He backhanded her across the face, making her see stars.

"Muzzle that one," he ordered.

Someone yanked her hair. When she gasped, a wooden dowel was thrust into her mouth and secured at the back of her head by vinyl straps. She kicked and thrashed but they just laughed at her.

"It ain't your turn yet, honey. Just settle down," the man in camo told Alexa before turning his attention to Crissy. After unclipping her handcuffs, he pulled her into a sitting position.

Alexa noticed the poor girl's eyes were glazed over and she looked confused.

"This is your big shot, honey. Make it believable." The man who'd ordered Alexa be gagged was speaking sweetly to Crissy. "Now in this scene, your husband has returned from war. You never expected to see him alive again. You can't wait to touch him. You have to make sure he's real and not another fantasy that you've had night after night. Your only thought is to please him and make up for all those lost months without him."

Crissy wore a huge grin and was brushing through her hair with her fingers. "Got it."

"If you do this right, you'll be a big star. Everyone will know your name." The man continued to prep her.

Alexa's heart sank. Whatever they'd given Crissy had completely befuddled her. She ran a finger across her teeth and pinched her cheeks. Alexa knew Crissy believed she was about to audition.

The man in jeans led Crissy to the lit area of the warehouse. "You're going to stand by the dresser.

When you see your husband, you run to him. You have to make it look real, Crissy. He's your husband and you missed him terribly."

"I understand." Crissy looked eager as she stood waiting. She ran her hands down her body as if smoothing out her clothes. She seemed to have no idea she was completely naked.

Tears rolled down Alexa's cheeks. Looking at the bed and Crissy's lack of attire, Alexa knew exactly what they had planned for the girl. Though Alexa continued to struggle, all she accomplished was shredding the skin around the handcuffs.

The man in jeans took his place behind a movie set camera then shouted action.

As the man in camo appeared under the lights, Crissy rushed to him. She threw herself into his arms and kissed him. He said something Alexa couldn't hear then Crissy fell to her knees and began unbuckling his belt.

A shadow fell across Alexa's face. She turned to watch her brother kneel down beside the cot. A feeling of cold dread washed over her.

"Why are you crying, Lexi? Upset because Crissy gets to go first?" He sneered down at her.

Alexa tried to breathe deeply and keep from panicking. Danny's eyes were soulless voids. His lips looked permanently curled into a cruel parody of a smile. He'd gained a few pounds, yet his face was gaunt. His hair was now more gray than brown. Time had not been his friend.

He turned to watch the scene play out. "Did you know she's fresh off the bus from Iowa? Yeah, I picked her out myself. Her dad's a pastor in some backward-ass town. I thought I was getting a virgin, but no. The cunt has a popped cherry." He shook his head.

"Damaged goods, barely worth all the time and trouble I've invested in her."

Danny rubbed his hand along his jaw as he scrutinized the couple on stage. "Damn, she's good at giving head. Look at that. His dick is halfway down her throat and still she's sucking him off. Huh, she'll serve us well."

"John, what dose did you give her?" Danny asked someone behind Alexa.

"Just five cc's. Imagine what will happen when we increase it."

"Fuckin' A." Danny turned back to Alexa. "We found a little concoction that'll take away inhibitions. In no time, she'll be addicted to the rush."

Alexa could just imagine what Danny had in store for Crissy and all the girls like her.

"This film is my insurance card." He waved Alexa's attention to the stage.

Crissy wrote, 'I'm daddy's little whore,' down her body in blood red lipstick.

"This 'audition' tape insures she'll keep her mouth shut and do as she's told. You'd be surprised what these girls will do to make sure their parents and friends never receive copies of it." Danny laughed as if it were all a big joke. "It's funny what bothers different girls. Some of them give in as soon as they see themselves up on the screen naked as the day they were born. Other's break down when they see the close-up of them getting their ass fucked while they scream for more. Each one has a different trigger, but they all cave in the end."

Alexa's stomach turned and she wished she could cover her ears. Her brother had always had a cruel streak, but she'd never expected him to sink to this level.

"She's a fairly smart girl. We'll lay out her options and she'll choose wisely. She'll have a roof over her head, a place to sleep and enough food to keep her alive." Danny turned his gaze back to Alexa. "And then there's you."

A shiver ran down her spine. Like being in the sights of a predator, she knew her life hung in the balance.

"You're as dumb as box of rocks. You don't even know when to die."

* * * *

A couple of hours ago, Sid had lost Alexa's signal completely. When Sammy had texted to say Grumer had had an allergic reaction to the narcotic cocktail they'd administered to get the truth out of the bastard, Sid had been tempted to go to critical care and force the answers out of him. Why the fuck hadn't he shot him full of Benadryl and gotten the information that they needed?

Sid felt like he was blindfolded with his hands tied behind his back and had been asked to create a museum quality copy of the Declaration of Independence. The penalty for failure was a firing squad. No, actually that would be preferable, because he didn't want to live in a world without Alexa.

Thanks to the terrorist assholes on 9/11, the flight restrictions were such that he couldn't just commandeer a helicopter and search until he picked up her trail. Nowadays it was impossible to do that covertly. He'd have to alert the local authorities, and since Desman had cops on the payroll, that wasn't an option.

He ran both hands through his hair and slammed his two-way radio against the side of the van. For the last couple of hours, Sid had been driving around the docks. Each unit had been given a different quadrant to search. They should have picked up a trace by now. He kept thinking they'd want her near the shipping lanes so Desman could get her out of the country quickly. What if that had never been his idea?

Being with the NBIA, he always thought in terms of crossing national borders, but what if Desman had plans for her here in this country? If Desman was just a paranoid SOB—and after the sustained drug use Sid had read about in his file that would make sense— maybe Desman hadn't suspected Alexa was working with law enforcement. Maybe he was following his normal routine.

He closed his eyes and concentrated. The answer was just outside his field of vision. He had the pieces of the puzzle, he just had to figure out how to assemble them.

Sid pulled his cell phone out, found the thumbnail picture of Teague and hit dial.

"Send me the addresses of all the warehouses Mr. G used." Through wiretaps and surveillance intel, they'd learned the crime family Desi was associated with had recently taken over Mr. G's remaining operations. Before Teague had laid claim to Chantel, the chief's daughter, Teague had taken out both G and his top enforcer. By working with Sammy and a few other uncover agents, Teague had been instrumental in closing several of G's human trafficking lines. Sadly, all he'd accomplished was slowing the ring down, not actually stopping it.

One of the most frustrating aspects of Sid's job was knowing that cutting off the head of the beast didn't mean the horror ended. More often than not, the monster just grew another, sometimes even more heinous than the original.

Teague been working non-stop to gather as much data as possible on the new boss. For the most part, it seemed they had continued the operations using the same buildings and equipment. Since Teague had a back door into their computers and they hadn't switched them out yet, Sid was hopeful they'd gather the needed evidence to put these assholes behind bars for the rest of their lives.

Within seconds, Teague had sent Sid the necessary information. Damn, the list was longer than Sid would have liked. One address stood apart from the others, though. It was only a couple blocks from Desman's Designs Studio. He remembered Alexa telling him a dirty cop had taken her to a warehouse the night of the fire. Could it be the same place?

It turned his stomach to think an officer of the law would recruit runaways for a sex slave ring, but he'd heard it happened. No occupation was free of bad seeds.

His next call was to Sammy. "I've got a possible location. I just sent you the address."

"I remember the place. G used to use it as a 'training facility' for the women. He used to make his snuff films there too," Sammy informed him.

"Sir, unit four has picked up her signal near Eighth Ave and Thirty-Seventh Street. I'm heading there now," his driver told him.

Finally, a real break. Eighth and Thirty-Seventh was about two blocks from G's warehouse.

"Are you listening to the radio chatter?" Sammy asked.

Sid reached over and turned the volume up. "It looks like the signal is coming from two different dumpsters."

Sid's stomach bottomed out. *Oh, God no.* It'd been hours. Anything could have happened in that span of time. The words 'snuff film' were swirling inside his brain. Had that been Desi's plan all along?

"Ray, go check it out."

Sid recognized the voice of Vincent, the agent in charge of the New York NBIA office.

An unprofessional groan told him 'Ray' was the rookie. He was also the only one dressed in a sanitation uniform, so it made sense to order him to go dumpster diving, but Sid didn't like leaving it to a greenhorn.

The sound of boots clanking as Ray climbed the side of the metal container rang loudly in Sid's ears.

"Oh, God," preceded a horrible bout of retching.

"Get him out of there before he destroys any evidence," Vincent barked into the radio.

Sid put a fist-sized dent into the side panel of the van he was riding in.

"We're three minutes out, sir," his driver advised.

* * * *

Danny's cruel smile turned Alexa's blood to ice. "I have special plans for you. A few years back, I tried to have you declared dead, but that asshole Hawkings threatened to hire private investigators to look for you. He never believed you killed Ezzy and set fire to the warehouse."

Now she knew why he was using an outside lawyer. Tears pooled in her eyes as she remembered the kind old man. Thank goodness Danny hadn't tried to harm him.

"I have it all planned out. In a few months, your body will be discovered. Aside from virgins, do you know what brings the highest dollar in hookers?"

She refused to acknowledge his question. It wasn't like she could answer with a gag in her mouth.

"Rape fantasies. I imagine that after being raped four or five times a day by any man who can front me enough money will take some of that extra meat off your bones and give your dead body the proper two-bit whore look that will send Hawkings into a not so early grave." Danny continued to taunt her.

"He's never cared much for me, but your picture still hangs in his office. If it weren't for the mandates in the fucking will, I'd have fired his ass and he knows it."

Crissy screamed, drawing both their attention. She was on her hands and knees while a dark-haired man was between her legs, slamming into her with such force it had to be excruciatingly painful.

"Smile for the audience, Crissy. Let your fans know how much you like your ass fucked," the cameraman encouraged.

Crissy turned toward the camera and her lips angled upward. Pain was etched in the lines of her face but she repeated the phrase. "I like to be ass fucked."

Alexa renewed her struggles to get free. Her heart was breaking for Crissy. She couldn't believe her own brother could be a part of something so cruel.

"There's no need to be jealous, Lexi. I've already got a few customers lined up for you. The first one paid me ten grand for three days. After he has his fill of you, he plans to whore you out to his friends and make up most of his fee. He warned me, they can be brutal." Danny shrugged. "The dumb-ass played perfectly into my hands. I told him he'd have to pay a little more since you'd be out of commission for a few days."

Danny laughed viciously and shook his head. "Like I'd let you lay on your ass and recuperate. What the fuck, does he think I run some kind of charity house?"

He grabbed the strap of the gag and leaned down within a few inches of her face. "You'll fuck whoever I say, whenever I say, regardless of the condition you're in."

Alexa's heart beat erratically. Danny was unhinged. He wasn't trying to scare her. He was simply sharing his plans.

"Toward the end, I figure the only dipshits willing to screw you will be those already infected with every venereal disease on the planet so it won't much matter. You're worth more to me dead than you are alive," he murmured as if to himself as he watched the stage.

Danny turned his full attention back to Alexa. "I just have to make sure I set the scene first. Within a week, begging for scraps of food will be second nature. Your stomach will shrink to where you couldn't eat a full meal even if it were given to you. A good night's sleep will be measured in minutes instead of hours. Just long enough for one customer to leave and another arrive."

Bile rose in her throat. She couldn't believe any human could have such a flagrant disregard for life, and to think he shared her DNA made her ashamed. What had happened to him?

"More, bitch. Let me hear you beg for it!" the man on stage with Crissy ordered.

"Fuck my ass harder, I love it," Crissy screamed for the cameras.

Alexa rolled as far over as she could with her hands cuffed to the cot and vomited what little she had in her stomach. The gag kept it from all leaving her mouth and she feared she'd choke to death. Shaking her head, she tried to drag in a gulp of badly needed air. Snot was running from her nose and tears ran down her cheeks.

Danny jumped out of range before she dirtied his shoes. He tossed a slew of curses at her before he disappeared into the shadows.

She wiped her face as best she could on the side of the thin mattress. No matter what the alternative was, she refused to be at Danny's mercy. Disregarding the agony, she forced the handcuffs farther up her arms. Bending her wrist till the pain sent stars dancing in her field of vision, she felt the catch. Just a little more and she'd be able to push enough to get loose.

The man on stage yelled as his body shook from an obvious orgasm. Alexa drew several deep breaths and demanded her stomach stop rolling. If she thought about poor Crissy, she'd never find the strength to escape.

"Perfect. That should do it," the cameraman advised.

"Someone needs to teach this bitch how to suck cock or we need to bust out a few of her teeth. She scraped me with her molar. I think I'm bleeding," complained the guy on stage. He climbed out of bed then tossed Crissy over his shoulder.

"How did I do?" Crissy asked softly as he dumped her back onto the cot and secured her hands.

"Don't worry, honey. You'll get better as time goes by. Now that we've got that tape made, we can take off the kid gloves and start your training in earnest." He grabbed his cock and examined it. "Son of a bitch. She scratched me good. Where's the god damn pliers? I'm ripping that tooth out."

Alexa cringed away from the man as her stomach rebelled again. With nothing left in her tummy to lose, she began to dry heave. Once she could catch her breath again, the man was gone.

Chapter Thirteen

Sid's phone buzzed. He looked down at Teague's face on the screen and hit the answer button. "Got something?" Sid asked, hopeful Teague had good news for him.

"Alexa's picture was uploaded to a sex trade site about an hour ago. Based on the computer's IP address, I think she's being held at G's training facility. I'll send you the coordinates."

Is it the phone connection or is there something off about Teague's voice?

"What aren't you telling me?" Sid asked, wondering if he really wanted to know.

A heavy sigh confirmed Sid's fears. "She's listed in the rape fantasy section. From what I've seen, that's basically a death sentence. We gotta get her outta there, man."

Sid's stomach plunged. Things were moving too fast. Just this morning he'd held her tight and promised her he'd protect her. His throat tightened as he hit the end button. He couldn't hear anymore. Sid pounded the side of the van again. "Hurry the fuck up!" he shouted at his driver.

The pinging sound from Sid's cell notified him he'd received Teague's text. A quick look confirmed it was the same warehouse Sid had suspected. It was also about two blocks away from the dumpster where Alexa's signal had been picked up and where they were in route to.

Sid's radio crackled to life. "False alarm, folks. Just a bunch of wigs and a mannequin from the cosmetology school around the corner. There's a bag of women's clothes in here too, along with enough fish carcasses to keep a brood of cats happy for a lifetime. We'll take the bag to the IT geeks, but I'd bet a week's salary they dumped her clothes in here and that's where the signal's coming from," Vincent informed the task force.

Relief overwhelmed Sid, causing a fine tremor to run the length of his body. His logical side kicked him in the ass. Just because the mannequin hadn't been Alexa didn't mean she was safe. He couldn't think about how vulnerable she was. If her clothes were in that bag, she didn't even have the shank they'd hidden in the heel of her shoe. An image of her huddled alone and naked popped into his head. It was enough to send him busting down every door in New York until he found her.

"Let's meet back at the office and we'll figure out where we go from here," Vincent suggested through the radio.

"Fuck that. There's every reason to believe she's being held at G's old training facility. We need to go in, before they move her. I'm sending out a weblink now. You have two minutes to log in. We'll go over the plan from there." Sid quickly set up the webcast and pulled all the intel Teague had been feeding him to create a simulated version of the warehouse.

* * * *

The lights over the stage were turned off, plunging the warehouse into darkness. Alexa heard the other girls whispering to each other, but she couldn't make out any of what they were saying. She'd planned her escape so many times, she had no doubt she could find the window without any trouble.

Alexa knew this was her best chance to get away. She shoved the handcuffs as far up her arms as she could maneuver them then forced her wrist to find the catch. On the third try, it sprang open. The metal clanking against the cot sounded unbelievably loud. She froze and counted to ten, waiting for the lights to click back on and the men to surround her. Reaching behind her head, she unlatched the clasp on the gag and spit it out.

A few more seconds ticked by before she eased her feet to the cement floor and crouched. The rush of cold reminded her she was still alive and she made a solemn vow to stay that way.

"Crissy, listen to me." Alexa's eyes were slowly adjusting to the low light. She could make out Crissy's form tossing and turning on the cot. "Your parents love you. Don't think that anything these men do will ever change that. Do you hear me? They will always love you."

She was obviously still under the effects of whatever drugs they'd given her, but maybe her words of encouragement would sink it. If something happened and Alexa didn't make it out, she wanted to give Crissy whatever help she could.

A whimper came from Crissy's direction. "I hurt."

She bent low near Crissy. "I'm going to get help. I promise I'll get you out of here as soon I can." Instead of a response, Crissy ground her legs together and rocked back and forth, seemingly unaware of Alexa.

As quickly but quietly as possible, Alexa made her way to the stage. She stayed in a crouch. Nearing the bed, she grabbed the shirt the man had discarded and slid her arms through it. The smell of tobacco and sweat hit her hard, but anything was better than being naked.

Alexa avoided the bed and headed directly toward the window.

"We're right outside, baby. We're coming for you," Sid's voice crooned into her earbud.

She gasped and her legs wobbled. He'd found her. She covered her mouth with her hand to keep a sob from escaping.

Suddenly, from all sides of the building, she heard loud crashes and banging. The lights came on and she saw smoke filling the building. Alexa pulled back the curtains and prepared to force the window open. Instead of the darkened alley she'd expected, a used red-brick wall met her gaze. It was a stage façade.

"You didn't really think I'd let you get away from me again, did you Lexi?" Danny taunted from behind her. His whiskey-laden breath assaulted her nose.

She turned to fight, but he gave her no room. Crowded against the wall, she had nowhere to go. Danny bent his knees and plowed his shoulder into her gut. The back of her head hit the bricks and she crumbled, fighting to breathe. She felt Danny's hands grabbing her thighs and she tried to push him away. He easily overpowered her and pulled her into a fireman's carry.

"Help!" she screamed, doubting anyone could hear her. Each step he took jarred her ribs, and blessed darkness hovered on the edges of her vision. All she had to do was reach for it and the pain would be gone.

"Describe your surroundings, Alexa." Sid's calm voice gave her a surge of energy.

How was she supposed to do that? Then she remembered a microphone was woven into the braid of her hair as a backup. "Danny, put me down. Let me go." She had to give Sid enough clues to understand what was going on without letting Danny know she was communicating with Sid.

Alexa continued to struggle, but Danny locked an arm around her legs, limiting her movement.

"Where are you taking me? It's dark down here. You know basements scare me, Danny. Please let me go," she pleaded with him.

"Shut the fuck up! We're being raided again, goddamn it. You haven't changed a bit. You're still a whiny little bitch." Danny was breathing hard as he navigated the steep stairs with her over his shoulder. "I'll knock you out if I have to."

"Find the door to the basement. He's taking her out that way," Sid advised the troops with him.

Alexa grabbed the banister and held on, knocking Danny off balance. He spun into the handrail, pinning her leg painfully between him the metal. He smashed his fist into her broken wrist then continued down the stairs.

She screamed in agony and fought to stay conscious. Dear God, it hurt.

"Alexa, baby, what happened? Talk to me," Sid whispered to her through their connection.

"I'm okay," she managed to get out without whimpering much.

Danny laughed. "Ha! I forgot you used to talk to yourself. I've got the cure for that. Pain. I've found when given in large enough doses words become too much trouble. Eventually the only sounds that you'll be making are screams and whimpers."

Alexa didn't doubt his knowledge of torture techniques. The brother she'd played hide and seek with in fabric stores while growing up was long gone. This man carrying her to a fate worse than death was a caricature of the worst things hidden in the human psyche.

They came to a halt and Danny bent down, allowing her tippy-toes to skim the ground. She heard the scraping of metal before he grabbed her shoulders and forced her down on her knees.

"Get your ass in there." He swatted her butt and shoved her.

"No tunnels, Danny. There are rats down there." She was also afraid her tenuous connection to Sid would be lost once she entered the tiny passageway.

Danny kicked her through the opening and she scrambled to get away from him. Her left wrist refused to bend or take her weight. His next kick sent her tumbling. Her teeth rattled as her shoulder and jaw crashed onto the ground.

The squeaks of rodents were loud as they protested the intrusion into their space. Their proximity was almost as frightening as Danny's. Alexa cradled her left arm against her stomach as she crawled as quickly as she was able.

Hope flared as she noticed how tight the tunnel was. She was small and flexible. Maybe she'd be able to put some distance between her and Danny. The rough concrete hurt her knees and it was almost impossible to keep her weight off her injured wrist, but she moved as fast as she could. As the sounds from Danny grew more faint, her optimism increased.

Alexa couldn't hear anything from Sid, and she prayed once she was above ground again their connection would come back.

As a light appeared ahead of her, she wondered where the passageway led. Would one of Danny's men be waiting for her? She'd been so focused on getting away from her brother and avoiding the rats, she hadn't noticed if the tunnel was straight or angled upward.

God, she hoped she'd be at street level once she reached the opening. Being enclosed in earth and concrete was a nightmare all its own.

Nearing the light, she saw the shaft opened into a storage room of sorts. Kegs of beer were lined up along one wall. Was it a bar or nightclub? If she screamed would anyone help her or would she just bring more vultures down onto her?

Before she could take the final step out of the tunnel, Danny grabbed her ankle and yanked, bringing her flat against the cold, dirty concrete.

"Don't even think you can get away from me, bitch." He slipped something tight around her ankle then punched her in the back of the thigh, giving her a charley horse that made it difficult to move.

Knowing he wanted to hear her cry out, she kept her grunt of pain locked between clenched jaws and scurried from the confined space.

* * * *

"Alexa! Alexa!" Damn it, their communications were severed again.

"Teague, he's taking her out through a tunnel. Get me all the information you can on the surrounding buildings. I need a direction," Sid ordered into his phone as he found a set of steps leading to the basement and took them two at a time. Her sharp exhale right before he'd lost her had him scared. The bastard had hurt her again.

He was setting himself up to get shot. The lighting sucked, if Desi had hidden away in a corner, he could have easily picked Sid off. There was no cover to speak of. Not that it mattered. Sid half wanted Desi to take a shot at him. It'd give Sid a direction to vent his anger.

Throughout the vast warehouse, they'd found twenty-three girls. A few were as a high as a kite and in Sid's opinion those were the lucky ones. Most showed signs of continued abuse. None of them looked like they'd eaten a real meal in a long time and Sid wouldn't even hazard a guess at the last time they'd been given a shower. To think that each one of those girls had a family and friends worried sick about them registered on a new level for him.

Sid continued checking the walls for any possible opening as he waited for Teague to point him in a direction.

"South is my best guess. There's a neighborhood tavern across the alley. The liquor license is sketchy at best. An elderly couple from Kansas City isn't likely to own controlling interest in a bar in New York. I suspect it's really owned by an associate of Desi's." Teague sounded as frustrated as Sid felt.

"I'm on it," Sammy joined in.

Sid hadn't been aware his friend had rejoined the search, but he was glad to have someone he trusted on Alexa's trail and covering his back.

He went to the south wall and quickly found the hastily covered tunnel entrance. Knowing he was being reckless as hell, he holstered his gun and dropped to his knees to charge through. The space was tight. Crawling on all fours had both the walls and ceiling brushing against him. At what he gauged was the halfway point between the two buildings, he thought he saw a glimmer of light up ahead. A noise sounded, but it was difficult to make it out. Each time he moved, his clothing scraped against the concrete.

He stopped in the shadows about a foot from the entrance. Two men stood near the doorway. Sid paused to listen. Though the men were quiet, Sid recognized one set of boots. They belonged to Sammy. He climbed out of the tunnel and refused to acknowledge the disappointment at not seeing Alexa.

"We must have just missed them." Sammy pointed to a few still wet drops of blood.

Sid's jaw tightened. He had little doubt who the splatters had come from. He pushed away his feelings of failure and desperation. There'd be time later for recriminations. Right now he had to keep his focus. Alexa was alive and he would find her.

"None of your fucking business, Albert. Give me the goddamn keys. I'll call you later."

Sid waved his hand for silence and pressed the bud in his ear in a little tighter.

"Get in the car."

"No! H—" A grunt of pain took the place of the rest of the word Alexa had tried to shout.

"They're getting into a car." Sid sprinted across the room and through the doorway. He headed toward the kitchen, praying Desi had taken her out the back. Near the stoves, he spotted another drop of blood, signaling he'd chosen correctly.

"Get in, Lexi. I'm sick of your shit." Desi's voice rang loud and clear through Sid's earpiece.

A sharp cry followed by the slamming of a door had Sid shoving the bar's employees out of the way as he searched for the rear entrance. Finding it, he threw his weight against the door's push bar, tossing it open with gusto.

A man Sid assumed was 'Albert' took a step back in alarm. One glance at the loaded Sig Sauer a few inches from his face and Albert put his arms in the air.

"Where's the girl?" Sid demanded.

"No habla ingles," Albert answered smugly.

Sid smashed the man's nose into his elbow and shoved the Sig Sauer into his mouth. "Maybe you *'habla'* Sig Sauer, then."

"Dude, we ain't got time for this. Just end him and let's go," Sammy reminded Sid.

Albert started to shake and a glossy wet stain began spreading across his black pants.

The van Sid had been using during the stake-out blocked off the alley entrance.

"Are you going to tell me what type of car they got into or do I blow your head off?" Sid asked with finality.

Albert put his hands in a begging position, which Sid interpreted to mean he'd spontaneously learned how to speak English. Testing his theory, Sid withdrew the pistol a few inches.

"White Taurus. Brand new. No plates."

"Get the hell out of here and if you call Desi and warn him, I'll come back. Trust me, you won't like how this ends." Sid, Sammy and the local NBIA agent took off running for the van.

Sid related the car information to the rest of the units and began searching the street cameras for any sight of it. It would have to be white. Every other motherfucking car was either white or silver.

He pressed the switch opening his private link to Alexa. "Baby, talk to me," he pleaded, needing to hear her voice.

"Sid?" Alexa sounded shocked to hear him.

He breathed a sigh of relief at the sound of her voice. "I'm here baby. Where are you?" He needed a direction or he was going to lose her again.

"Sid, don't leave me. It's dark and I hate the dark."

The road noise coming through their connection was louder than it should have been. Sid looked out the van's windshield. With all the street lights and other cars going by, it wasn't all that dark. He must have shoved her in the trunk.

"I know. We'll fill our bedroom with candles so it's never dark again." Though he wanted nothing more than to comfort her, he needed some idea where they were heading. "Do you know where he's taking you?"

"No. He said he had customers lined up." She whimpered. "They paid him so they can rape me."

Sid imagined her huddled on the trunk floor with her chin quivering as her voice broke. He slammed his fist several times into the side of the van.

"Breaking your hand won't help us locate her, Sid. Find your happy place, man."

He flipped Sammy off.

"He said he was going to keep me alive until I looked like a two-bit whore then he was going to kill me and leave my body where Mr. Hawkings can find it." Alexa was talking softly, but he heard her clearly enough.

He suspected she'd pulled her braid containing the microphone nearer to her mouth.

"He drugged Crissy and tricked her into making a porn movie. If she doesn't do what he wants, he'll send copies to her friends and family. You have to stop him, Sid. Don't let him keep ruining people's lives."

"*We* will stop him, Alexa. You and me together." He didn't like the way she sounded, almost as if she'd given up.

"I won't be raped. Not again, Sid. I'd rather die first."

Now it was his turn to beg. "Don't leave me, Alexa. You own my heart, baby. You live, for me. For us. Don't throw our chance away. No matter what, you fight to live."

For the longest time all he heard was road noise, then finally she answered, "I'll try."

Sid let out a breath he hadn't realized he'd been holding.

"We're slowing down, I think."

Oh God, the connection was breaking up again. He got on the radio and started barking orders. If the chief were here, he'd have already relieved Sid of command. He knew he'd lost all pretense of professionalism.

"I'm scared...I..."

He couldn't make out the words.

She sounded like she was underwater. "Not again."

The road noise stopped and Sid feared they'd lost their link. "Stop the van. Turn it around. Head back in the direction we were coming from."

For long moments, only silence came through their com link.

"Oww, Danny, that hurts." Alexa's voice sounded tired but strong.

"Like I give a shit. Get your ass out of there. Time for you to start earning your keep."

"Danny, there's glass. I don't have shoes. Danny!"

Alexa's groans of pain shot through Sid until his vision was a haze of red. Once he found Desi, he was going to kill him, slowly and with great malice.

"Little Dick's Inn?" Alexa asked incredulously.

"Welcome to your new home away from home until the fallout from the raid calms down."

"Little Dick's Inn, is that the name of a motel?" Sid asked over the radio.

Some scraping sounds came over the link. "Get your ass moving," Desi ordered.

"I've got glass in my feet, quit shoving me," Alexa pleaded.

"In a few hours that will be the least of your concerns, I assure you," Danny responded gruffly.

"I know that place. It's a flea bit motel a few miles east of us. Heading there now, sir," his driver reported before he tossed the van into a sharp turn and floored it.

Chapter Fourteen

Danny had said 'in a few hours'. Did that mean she was fairly safe for the time being? She prayed that was the case.

"Get on the bed," Danny ordered.

"Please don't do this, Danny. You're my brother. Why do you want to hurt me?" If Sid had heard her say the name of the motel, she knew nothing would stop him from finding her.

"Oh, bitch, please. Don't waste your breath. The only loyalty I have is to money and right now you're standing between me and a substantial piece of the trust fund."

Alexa sat on the bed, relieved to have the weight off her bleeding feet. She looked at the door only a few feet away and wondered if she could reach it before he grabbed her again.

"We're on the way, baby. Hang on. Just keep him talking," Sid reassured her.

Danny pulled open the drawer of the nightstand and retrieved two pairs of handcuffs. Since neither had the custom-made quick-release catch, it wouldn't be possible for her to escape once he put those on her.

"I'll sign it over to you. Just let me go, Danny. I've never told anyone about Ezzy. I'm sure it was an accident anyway."

He snorted. "Like hell! I beat her brains in using the fire extinguisher. Dumb bitch thought she could order me around."

Maybe if she fed his ego, he'd keep talking. "She didn't understand that Mom and Dad meant for you to run the company the way you thought was best. She just thought you were an upstart." *Please forgive me, Ezzy.*

"What?" Danny slipped one cuff from each set around the brass bars of the headboard. "You can't really be that stupid, can you? What am I saying? Of course you are. Mom and Dad were about to change their will. I had to get rid of them before Dad signed the updated version Hawkings sent over for them."

Danny couldn't have hurt her more had he tried.

Sid's soft voice centered her. "I'm sorry, baby. Stay focused and keep him talking. Just breathe in and out for me. You can do this."

I might be able to, but I don't want to. I want to just lie down and die. Danny shares my genes. Is there a monster hidden inside of me too?

"Damn, if I'd known that's all it took to shut you the hell up, I'd have told you first thing." He grabbed her broken wrist and hauled her to the top of the bed then cuffed her there.

Alexa had tried to remain stoic, but the pain blinded her. She screamed as stars danced in her field of vision. Before she could catch her breath, he'd handcuffed her right wrist as well.

"Rest while you can Lexi, Fuller is an evil bastard. You've got a rough evening ahead of you." Danny laughed as he closed the door behind him.

"Baby, are you all right?" Sid asked softly, as if he was afraid of her answer.

"He's gone." She'd failed to keep him there and she had no idea where he was headed. Undoubtedly, he was off to ruin someone else's life.

"No worries, baby. We got all the evidence we need to lock him away for the rest of his life. We're about two minutes out. Keep talking to me. I need to hear your voice. Do you know what room you're in?"

"One hundred nineteen. The last room on the end." She was oddly numb. Oh, her wrist hurt like a son of a bitch, but she felt dead inside. "Sid?"

"We're pulling in now."

"I don't want anyone to see me like this. Can you come in alone?" She tried to curl into a ball, but the glass shards impaled her feet and sent pain shooting up her legs every time she moved them.

* * * *

"Don't do it, man."

"No way."

"Absolutely not."

"It could be a trap."

Pretty much every person on the team chimed in, but Sid didn't give a damn. He knew Alexa would have found a way to warn him if it had been a set-up.

"Of course, Alexa. Tell me something, baby. What's your favorite color? Red?" he asked as they pulled into a parking spot a building away but with the room in clear view.

"No, not red. Right now, it's thundercloud gray."

She sounded so sad it broke his heart. He'd fucked up this mission from start to finish.

"Dude, you can't go charging in there alone." Sammy put his body between Sid and the van doors.

Sid didn't bother to answer him, he just glared Sammy in the eye until his friend moved out of the way.

"Can you open the door?" He assumed she'd been restrained in some manner, but the more intel he had the better.

"No. He handcuffed me to the bed."

Her tone surprised him. He'd expected to hear relief or impatience in her voice instead she sounded resigned or maybe ashamed. He didn't want to think about what Desi may have done to her over the last few hours.

"Look around for me, baby. Do you see any cameras?" If he could help it, he didn't want Desi to know they'd found Alexa.

"I don't think so. I can't see the whole room, though."

Sid stalked toward the room with his Sig Sauer at the ready. As he approached the door, he was joined by two local agents and Sammy. Broken bottles littered the asphalt and fresh blood plotted a trail across the sidewalk. A new wave of anger pounded in his temples. "Do not enter the room until I give the all clear."

"That's not protocol, sir," one of the agents argued.

"I'm ranking AIC. If you've got a bitch with something, take it up with the chief and get the hell out of my way." He wasn't budging on this. Alexa hadn't asked him for much and he refused to let her down.

Sid tested the door but found it locked.

"Is that you, Sid? Someone's at the door," Alexa whispered in a panic.

"It's me, baby. You're fine." He pulled out a tiny but strong shim stick from the pack of tools attached at his belt and jimmied the lock. Sid gave the room a cursory glance before his attention fell to the bed. His chest constricted at the sight of her. The cast was missing and her wrist lay at an unnatural angle. Her face was scraped and bruised. Fresh tears dotted her cheeks. Red, angry marks covered most of her body and both feet were bleeding.

He immediately went to her and wrapped her in the coverlet before yelling, "All clear," to the waiting agents.

In short order, the room filled with fellow law enforcement officers.

"My sweet angel, are you okay?"

Alexa ducked her head as if attempting to hide.

He blocked her from view as best he could. "Get me some bolt cutters," he snapped to the closest agent. It was imperative he get her medical treatment.

"The key might be in there." Alexa nodded toward the nightstand. "He pulled the handcuffs out of the drawer."

Their eyes locked for a brief moment before she turned away.

Was there censure in her glance? He certainly deserved it. He'd promised to keep her safe and just look at her. He'd failed her.

Sid opened the drawer by pulling on the bottom corner. It was filled with well used sexual instruments. His stomach revolted at the idea of any of them coming near Alexa. He pushed his anger down. Toward the back, he found two keys on a slip ring.

"Did you get the rest of the girls out? They drugged Crissy and..." She broke down into tears.

He worked the keys and released her from the handcuffs then immediately swung her into his arms and headed to the van. "She's at the hospital." Sid didn't know which girl was 'Crissy', but they were all being checked out. Some of the women were in pretty bad shape.

Sid heard the crunching of boots on the gravel keeping pace with him. He peered over his shoulder and saw Sammy was right behind him. Sid could always count on him. As soon as Sid stepped through the sliding door, he heard it slam shut. A moment later, Sammy took the driver's seat.

"ER?" his friend asked.

"Yes," Sid answered before nuzzling his cheek against Alexa's hair. "I'm so sorry, baby. I never thought this would happen."

"This wasn't your fault, Sid. I could have called a stop to it as soon as Danny sent someone else to the storage unit, but I made the decision to ride it out." She sniffled and lowered her voice. "He's evil, Sid. Truly evil. I'd held out hope that someone else was forcing him to do these things, that maybe he'd just got in too deep with gambling debts or something." She shook her head. "No one's forcing him. He's twisted."

"I know, baby. Every agent on the eastern seaboard is looking for him. We'll get him," he assured her.

"He was sending a man and his friends to rape me. As soon as he gets there and finds me gone, he'll contact Danny. If my brother suspects the police are looking for him, he'll disappear," she warned him.

"We have a female agent who's going to take your place. When Fuller shows up, he'll be arrested. He won't have the opportunity to tip off Desi."

Alexa looked up at him sharply. "No. Absolutely not. He'll hurt her, Sid. Don't you dare put anyone else at risk. I'll go back if I have to."

"Like hell you will. There will be agents just a few feet away. She'll never be alone." He'd promised Alexa the same thing. He'd told her he'd be just outside and all she had to do was say 'parents' to bring the whole team to her rescue. No way could she have any faith in his reassurances after what had happened to her. "We won't fail her, Alexa. Not like we did you." He gripped her a little harder.

The van bounced over a curb and Alexa hissed in pain as it rolled to a stop. Sammy jumped out and opened the side door before rushing inside to get help.

As carefully as possible, Sid eased them out of the vehicle. Seconds later, Sammy and an intern met them with a wheelchair.

"I've got her," Sid informed them. It was irrational, but he wasn't ready to let go of Alexa. His strides were long as he carried her through the automatic doors. Sid didn't know what Sammy had told them, but he was immediately ushered into a room. As much as he wanted to continue holding her, he knew he had to give the doctor some space. Reluctantly, he set her down on the exam table.

"Sir, you can wait just outside the door or in the lobby if you prefer," the nurse, a plump woman with a permanent scowl, informed him.

"No," both he and Alexa answered at the same time.

"If he can't stay with me then I'm leaving." Alexa moved to jump off the table.

Sid blocked her path. "I'm not going anywhere. You need to be checked out. Just settle down, baby." He was a fine one to talk. He'd been ranting like a lunatic most the evening.

The nurse glared at him and pointed to the end of the bed.

Alexa kept her attention on Sid as they peeled back the coverlet from that nasty motel. The nurse immediately covered her in heated blankets, but she couldn't stop shivering. Intellectually she knew it was simply her body's reaction to shock, but she saw her inability to control it as another failure.

Two lines seemed permanently stationed on Sid's forehead. She didn't remember seeing them before. His lips were pursed as well. She couldn't decide if he was angry or worried.

She closed her eyes and tried to force her body to stop trembling. As soon as she lost sight of Sid, she became hyper aware of every touch, the blood pressure cuff squeezing her arm, someone pushing downward on her chin, forcing her to open her mouth, the doctor twisting her foot closer to the light. Without realizing what she was doing, she flailed her arms and tried to move off the bed.

"Restrain her," the doctor ordered, after being kicked in the face. He slid his wheelie chair a few feet away, holding his right cheek.

"No." Sid moved to her side. "Just give her a minute. She's been through a traumatic experience."

"We have to be able to work. I won't risk my staff being injured," the doctor countered. His dark brown eyes glared at her as if she'd kicked him on purpose.

"I'm sorry. It won't happen again." Alexa hated the pleading tone in her voice.

Another man, about twenty-five years old, with shaggy blond hair and dressed in hospital attire, entered the room with a camera and began taking photos. The flash sent another round of panic coursing through her. She looked up at Sid through teary eyes and tightened her hold on his hand.

"It's for evidence, baby." Sid crouched beside her. "Just focus on me."

"They photographed us," she whispered to him in explanation.

Something gripped her ankle and instantly she was back in the tunnel. She jerked away, needing to get free before Danny could hit her again.

"Look, asshole, don't you see the welts on her leg. They weren't put there during a walk in the park. If you aren't capable of even a modicum of compassion then get someone else in here." Sid was standing at full height and leaning protectively over Alexa.

The doctor looked as if he'd eaten something sour. "I'm almost finished. Just keep her still for a few more minutes."

Sid cupped his hand around the back of her neck and scrunched down to her level. "Just relax, Alexa. I'm here with you. It's all over."

But it wasn't. Danny was still out there and until he was behind bars, she'd never be safe.

The warm blanket was pulled off her and the nurse began cutting away the shirt she was wearing. She could feel the stares of the hospital staff then the flashes of the camera started going off rapid-fire.

"Alexa, look at me," Sid ordered. "Keep your focus on me."

"We need you to turn over, Alexa," the nurse told her as she began lowering the head of the table.

Once the table was flat, the nurse supported the board strapped to Alexa's left wrist. "Let me hold this above your head so you don't try to put any weight on it. Now roll toward your friend."

Alexa felt the sheet underneath her be pulled at the same time she moved, keeping her in virtually the same spot. Someone removed the shirt shortly before the camera started clicking again. She wished the earth would open up and swallow her whole. She could just imagine what she looked like. There wasn't a place on her body that didn't ache.

Sid moved to the head of the bed and fed her ice chips. Until they could ascertain the extent of her injuries, they wouldn't allow her to eat or drink anything.

"Are you still in touch with the team? Do you know if that man showed up yet?" She couldn't stop thinking about the female agent taking her place. It didn't feel right to allow someone else to put themselves at risk.

Sid turned his head slightly and showed her his earpiece. It was larger than hers since there was no reason for secrecy on his part. "Not yet. Everything is set-up and ready. There won't be any mistakes this time. Put it out of your head, Alexa."

Alexa felt something cold being dabbed on various parts of her back. As uncomfortable as that was, she preferred it to them taking photos of her. "I can't, Sid. He's going to run and we'll never catch him."

"We'll catch him, Alexa," Sid assured her.

"Okay, sweetie, let's get down to imaging. After a quick scan we'll get this wrist set." The nurse put her hand on Alexa's shoulder and helped her turn over. She reached into a drawer and pulled out a gown. "Let me help you guide your arm through."

Sid took one arm and the nurse took the other. Once she was covered she felt a little better.

"Come with me, Sid."

"I'm right beside you, babe. You're not getting rid of me." He linked his fingers through hers and caressed the back of her knuckles as they rode the elevator down to the basement.

"You'll have to wait outside while they take the scan, but it won't take more than a minute or two. We have the latest and greatest model," the technician advised them.

Sid started to say something but Alexa gripped his hand harder. "It's okay. I don't want you exposed to the radiation."

"I don't mind, Alexa. If you need me, I'm there," Sid offered.

She shook her head. She could do this. As soon as she let go of his hand, they wheeled her through the doors.

"You're so brave, baby. You make me proud." Sid used their link to talk to her.

"I'm not allowed to talk. Shhh." She giggled.

She lay perfectly still while the machine moved over her. The bright light reminded her of all the life after death stories she'd heard and jogged her memory on something Danny had said.

"You're worth more to me dead than alive. I just have to set the scene first." Danny didn't want her to quietly disappear. He needed her body to be discovered.

Once she was wheeled back to Sid, she sat up on her right elbow. "I know how to catch him."

Chapter Fifteen

"What the hell kind of scam are you trying to run on me, Desman?" Fuller shouted into the phone as he sat at a table with Sid, Sammy and Alexa in the motel room at the Little Dick's Inn. "Not only do I want a refund, you better include a hefty bonus since you've stuck me with doing your dirty work." He smirked at the NBIA agents sitting around the table with him.

"Fuck you. You ain't getting your money back." Desi sounded indignant.

"I ain't no necrophiliac, asshole. I'm not sticking my dick in a corpse. You absolutely will give me my fucking money back," Fuller demanded, his enormous face taking on a ruddy hue as he got into his role. "And people saw me coming in here so now I've got to make her disappear. That's your job. Since I'm doing your shit work, you can bloody well pay me."

"Son of a bitch. You killed her already? Motherfucking, cocksucker, what the fuck? I didn't want her dead yet. I haven't got my money's worth outta her. You owe me, big time," Desi countered.

Sid's stomach rolled at the casual way they were discussing Alexa's supposed death. He had the desire to pull out his Sig and end Fuller here and now. It didn't matter that Alexa was alive and sitting beside him. He'd come way too close to losing her to listen to shit like this.

"Whoa, I didn't kill her. I found her that way. Here I was expecting a weekend of fun and now I've got a mess to clean up. You owe me for that, Desman. As soon as it's dark, I'll make sure she disappears for good. Ain't nobody gonna find that body, but I want a full refund and a freebie," Fuller argued as he wiped the sweat dotting his forehead

"She was a little worse for wear, but very alive when I left her. Don't think you can fuck me over, Fuller. Yeah, I see what you're doing. You're gonna make her disappear all right. You're gonna keep her all for yourself. Well, bullshit." Desi was clearly furious. "I'm on my way and she better be there when I get there or I'll be coming after you next."

The line went dead and Fuller sat back in his chair. "That went well. Now what else can I do for you?" he asked while he ran his fingers up and down his lighter.

"Stand up and put your hands behind your back," Sid informed him.

"Now wait a minute. I did exactly as you asked. So I'm gonna just walk outta here and we'll both forget we ever saw each other." Fuller tensed and scooted closer to the exit.

Sid had searched the bag Fuller had brought with him. The implements he'd found inside had made his blood run cold. Fuller, and every man like him, deserved a special place in hell, and Sid would be more than happy to send him straight to it.

Alexa placed a hand on Sid's biceps. He wasn't sure what exactly he'd done to broadcast his thoughts, but Alexa's touch helped him breathe away a little of his anger. "Fuller, you have two choices." Sid lifted his index finger. "You can stand and put your hands behind your back or" — he added his middle finger — "I can tie you to the bed and test out some of the toys you brought in that bag of yours and we can carry you out of here tomorrow on a stretcher. Honestly, I hope you choose the second."

Fuller lost a shade or two of his spray-on tan. "Look, this was all just a bit of fun. I wasn't going hurt anyone."

"So, your choice is number two." He nodded. "Sammy..."

"No, no way, man." Fuller stood and looked longingly toward the door.

Sammy hit Fuller squarely between the shoulder blades with enough force to send him into the wall.

Alexa scurried into the restroom.

Sid covered Sammy while he cuffed Fuller and handed him off to two local field agents.

"Come on out, baby. It's just me and Sammy." He hated having her out of his sight and didn't expect that to change anytime soon. She really should be in the hospital, but she had been adamant about seeing this through.

Alexa opened the door and hesitantly walked to him at the small table. Her delicate body was covered in bruises and bandages.

"I'll go hang out on the roof." Sammy reached for the knob.

"No, don't go. It's all right." Alexa waved him to the padded chair on the far side of the bed.

Sammy looked to Sid before moving.

"Keep us company. Your ghost shirt isn't going to keep your brains from being baked on the rooftop," Sid teased his friend. There was nothing to do now but wait for Desi to show.

Alexa looked at Sid sharply. "Don't make light of his sacred beliefs. Just because you might not understand or believe in it doesn't mean you have the right to discount it."

Sammy laughed. "She's definitely your *better* half, dude." He sat down in the chair and propped his feet on the end of the bed. "Good luck teaching him any manners, Alexa. He may know what tie to wear with what jacket and what wine to sip with what food, but culturally he's ignorant."

The corner of her mouth twitched and a faint pink touched her cheeks for a moment.

"Many cultural traditions or beliefs can be linked in one way or another to a sound scientific theory," Alexa explained.

Sid snorted rudely. "No scientific theory I've ever heard of touts cotton fibers as being strong enough to stop bullets."

"I'll let the record stand for itself," Sammy retorted smugly.

Sid flipped him off.

"What record? What are you two talking about?" Alexa asked. She tapped her foot and immediately grimaced.

"I've been in the line of fire as often as Sid, but I don't carry around any souvenirs like he does."

"You're just a lucky bastard," Sid grumbled as he rubbed Alexa's thigh. Every movement she made seemed to bring her pain.

"Or he ducks better than you do," Alexa teased Sid. "I know watching Hackman shoot you ruined my whole day." Underneath the table she wrung her hands.

Both men burst out laughing. Sid was filled with pride. That Alexa was making the effort to joke with them after the experience she'd just gone through showed him just how strong she was. The tension was getting to her, but she kept up the banter.

Sid gently brushed two fingers over her injured cheek. "Perhaps we both need to get a little better at it."

"Couldn't hurt," she conceded.

"How much pain are you in, babe?" Sid wondered if she'd acknowledge it.

She shrugged. "The waiting is getting to me. How do you guys handle it?"

"You should have seen him while you were MIA. I thought he was going to have a stroke." Sammy poked fun at Sid again. "Papa threatened to have him relieved if he didn't get a grip."

Alexa leaned into Sid. "I'm sorry I worried you." She glanced at Sammy. "Who is Papa?"

"Teague is married to the chief's daughter, Chantel. When he's out of earshot, that's what he calls the boss," Sid explained.

At the mention of Teague's name, the tentative smile faded from Alexa's face. She wasn't ready to forgive him. His girl could definitely hold a grudge.

"Did I get you in trouble?" she asked Sid with concern etched in her expression.

"Sid and the chief are pretty tight, Alexa. He'd have to do more than bark orders like an idiot and piss off all the locals to get in any serious trouble. Besides, I'm sure Teague was running interference for us. I know you're mad at him, but he is one of the good guys," Sammy answered, sparing Sid the embarrassment.

"A white Taurus just pulled into the parking lot," one of the guys on the roof radioed. "He's circling around. Looks like this is it. Identify and notify."

"Grumpy's a go," Sid responded immediately.

"Hang tough, Alexa," Sammy told her as he slid out the bathroom window. A moment later a thud sounded on the roof above them. "Du-rag's a go," Sammy chimed in.

While the rest of the team readied for action, Sid turned his attention to Alexa. "Go into the other room."

"No. I'm staying with you. We'll see this through together." Her jaw tightened and her eyes locked with his.

By the look on her face, he knew nothing he said would change her mind. He'd never been more proud of her.

In the same motel room where Danny had left her to be raped, Alexa waited to face him one more time. She stood straight and tall in her kitten heels, ignoring the pain from the cuts on her feet. She smoothed out her pencil skirt and forced a pleasant expression on her face. Danny would never see weakness from her again.

Her heart beat double time as the chime signaled the door was unlocked. Sid stood in front of her with his pistol drawn. A few inches of the doorway were illuminated.

"What the..." Danny started to ask just as Sammy, holding onto the walkway awning, swung feet first directly into Danny's back. The door bounced off the wall and Danny landed face first on the floor of the motel room.

Sammy placed his knee against Danny's spine and his Glock at the back of his head. "Don't even think about moving."

Sid stepped forward and covered Sammy while he searched her brother. He found a small pistol in an ankle holster and bags of various colors and shapes of pills. He also found a packet of white powder and a mini spoon.

"I'm so glad you decided to join us again, Danny. You ran off so quickly we didn't really have a chance to discuss your future." Alexa spoke with a calm confidence she really didn't feel.

All three men stared at her for a moment. Sid was the first to grin and if she wasn't mistaken, he'd sent Sammy a conspiratory wink. Danny just glared at her as if seeing her for the first time.

She waved to the table. "Please, have a seat."

"What the hell is this all about?" Danny blustered as he got to his feet.

"The lady asked you to have a seat. I strongly advise you to do so." Sid kept his Sig Sauer trained on Danny's head as Sammy shoved her brother into the seat nearest the door.

Alexa took the farthest chair and sat at an angle, hiding the injured side of her face in the shadows and her cast under the table. "You see, Danny, these gentleman believe you have value to them. After our encounter, I fear they are wrong. In my opinion you're nothing more than a parasite that needs to be exterminated."

"Like I give two shits what you say."

Sammy smacked him upside the head. "Listen to your sister, asshole. She obviously got the brains in your family."

"You murdered Mom and Dad, Ezzy, Blanca and Marge."

"Who the fuck are Blanch and Marge? Worthless fucking bolts?" Danny asked indignantly.

Her stomach rolled at his callous disregard for human life. "*Blanca* and Marge were seamstresses who were trapped in the fire you set to hide the fact that you murdered Ezzy."

He waved his hand dismissing her. "That doesn't count. I was trying to kill you. They were just collateral damage, as the saying goes."

"As I was saying, you murdered five people that I'm aware of. I suspect there are others. While nothing you do to make amends will bring those people back, these gentleman believe you could serve a greater purpose working for them than rotting in a prison cell. I completely disagree. In the big picture of life, I think it would be very fitting if you were to spend your remaining days on this earth as an inmate's fuck toy."

Danny's eyes widened and his jaw dropped.

Sammy snorted and Sid's mouth twitched slightly before he regained his professional demeanor.

"I *sincerely* hope you refuse to help these men, or prove to be as useless as I believe you to be because I've been promised the opportunity to choose your bunkmate and I'm really looking forward to it." She watched Danny shift uncomfortably in his chair.

"What is she talking about?" He looked from Sid to Sammy then back to Sid.

"We have enough evidence to lock you away for several lifetimes, and with the gracious help we've received from Hackman, Grumer and Fuller, you'll never walk free again. Your associates decided to buy their way out of jail by supplying us information about you and your business dealings." Sid embellished the truth. "In the big scheme of things, you're just a small fry, and we're after bigger fish."

Danny ran a shaky hand through his slicked back, gray hair. His cocksure smile disappeared as his shoulders sagged. "What exactly are you offering?"

Sid shrugged. "That would depend on what you can tell us. I'll be honest with you. It won't be easy to wipe the slate clean. The last time I checked, the district attorney felt he had a rock solid case on thirteen counts of murder, and I lost track of the number of kidnapping, racketeering and other charges."

Alexa watched as the wheels began to turn for Danny. His rapid eye movement told her he was considering his options. The fact that he hadn't balked at Sid's bluff of thirteen murders made her wonder just how many people he was actually responsible for killing.

"What if I gift wrap Bobby the Bull for you?" Danny offered.

Are they really serious with these ridiculous names? Alexa wondered.

Sid looked at Danny incredulously. "Give me a break. Hackman sold out Bobby a week ago. We want DeRege." Hackman had been dead by then, but Danny didn't know that.

The blood drained from Danny's face and he shook his head. "Not the King. I'd rather go to prison." He stretched out his legs and grinned smugly. "Hell, I can file so many motions I won't go to trial until I'm old and gray."

Alexa fist pumped. "Yes! You hold to that line of thinking, Danny. That's exactly what you should do." She leaned back in her chair and smiled like it was Christmas morning. "You know, I've made millions as an interior decorator. I really have no need for our trust fund. I think I'll spend it on Viagra for your bunkmate." She'd only stretched the truth a little.

"You vindictive bitch." The vein on the side of his temple bulged. "We can do business, but I'm not talking to her anymore. If you want my help" — he tossed his chin in her direction—"then get her outta here."

That Danny thought he was in a position to make demands floored her. He must consider his crimes of little consequence.

"I think it's time to move this discussion down to headquarters," Sid announced.

Sammy opened the door. Several local agents entered and led Danny from the room.

Sid and Alexa stood on the sidewalk and silently watched. She knew he had to be locked away, but it still broke her heart. How the little red-headed boy her parents had dearly loved could have grown into such a monster, she'd probably never figure out.

An NBIA, white transit van was parked in the second row of spaces. The side door was slid open and Danny was stepping into it as he kicked off on the running board, knocking the agent to the left of him off balance. Danny grabbed the officer's pistol, turned and pointed it directly at Alexa.

Before she could register what was happening, Sid, Sammy and two local agents all opened fire, striking Danny several times about the head and chest. As if in slow motion, he crumpled to the ground.

* * * *

As the elevator doors of the New Yorker Hotel opened, Sammy clapped Sid on the back and headed off to his room.

Once they were alone, Sid turned to Alexa. "Your feet have to be hurting. Let me carry you."

She shook her head and walked to the room they shared.

In the couple of hours since the shooting, Alexa had barely said a handful of words. He'd been shocked when she had taken the lead with Desi, but she'd pushed just the right buttons. He'd been convinced Desi was ready to cooperate.

After sliding the plastic card into the slot, Sid held the door open for Alexa. He'd allowed the silent treatment while they'd been around other people, but now that they were alone, that shit was coming to an end.

He worked the lock, ensuring their privacy, and turned in time to watch her curl into a ball on the armchair near the desk. There wasn't a doubt in his mind that she'd avoided the couch to keep a distance between them.

"I'm going to run a bath for us." He waited a moment, but when she didn't reply he headed to the restroom.

Once the tub was filling, he returned to her side. "Babe, you need to give me some direction. I don't know what you need. Your sorrow is beating at me."

She looked up at Sid with tear-filled eyes. "I pushed him too hard. I wanted to show him how tough I was, that he couldn't break me." She sniffled.

"That's bullshit. If you have to blame someone besides the bastard himself, then blame me. I'm the one who shot him." And no matter how many crimes Desi committed, he was still her brother.

"You did nothing wrong, Sid. Once he had a hold of the gun, you had no choice. All you did was protect me and your team."

He sent up a silent prayer of thanks that Alexa realized that. "Come on, babe, let's get you into the bath. It's been a horrible couple of days."

Sid waited for a few moments. When she didn't respond, he picked her up and carried her to the tub. He nudged off her shoes before sliding her feet to the ground. She reached behind her and unfastened her skirt, allowing it to pool at her ankles while Sid unbuttoned her shirt and pushed it from her shoulders. Alexa added her bra to the pile as Sid turned off the water.

He offered his hand to help guide her into the tub. As she sat down, he wrapped her cast in a towel and rested it on the edge. He used one of the complimentary cups to douse her hair. Taking his time, he massaged her scalp with shampoo.

Her soft coos eased a few of the knots in his stomach. At least he could do this right.

"I love your hair. It's thick and gorgeous." He needed to find something safe to talk about.

"It hid the microphone pretty well. I'm grateful for that."

So much for finding a neutral subject. "We found the other one in a dumpster a couple of blocks from the warehouse." The emotions of those few hours came rushing back. "I've never been so worried." He rinsed out the shampoo then applied the cream rinse.

"I can't imagine what it must have been like for you. I was wrong to put you through that." She tipped her head back and closed her eyes while he took care of her.

He wasn't entirely sure he'd heard her correctly. She'd been through hell and here she was apologizing that he'd been scared? It was obvious Alexa was taking the blame for the mission deviating from the plan.

"Babe, I was running the operation. It was my decision. Why don't you tell me what's been going on inside that brain of yours." He was convinced it was more than grieving.

Alexa was quiet for so long he assumed she wasn't going to answer him.

When he noticed her staring at her water-soaked fingers, he asked, "Are you ready to get out?"

She nodded and stood up. He wrapped her in a towel and carried her to the bed, feeling utterly helpless.

After drying off, she twisted her hair into a loose bun and lay down.

Sid left the bathroom light on, knowing Alexa wouldn't want it completely dark, then curled around and pulled the covers over them. He settled in, knowing it was going to be a long night. He wondered if he should put in a call to the agency shrink he'd worked with on a few cases. He had no idea if he should push her to talk or just comfort her.

"He hurt me," Alexa softly whispered.

He tightened his arms around her and waited to see if she'd continue.

"Instead of crumbling, I got mad. That's not normal is it? He killed our parents and destroyed my childhood. I should have been overwhelmed by grief but once the shock passed, all I could think about was getting even with him. I wanted him in jail." Her voice was growing louder. "When you told me the FBI and the DEA wanted him as an informant, I was so angry. I wanted him to spend the rest of his life behind bars." Alexa was trembling.

"Baby, anger is the second stage of grief. It's perfectly normal," he assured her.

"Not like this. It was all-consuming. I wanted to hurt him, just like he'd hurt me."

"I don't understand. What are you telling me, Alexa?"

"The memories I have of my dad are those of a child. He was larger than life. When the loneliness would get to be too much, I'd scour the libraries and later the Internet and read every article I could find about my parents. They all describe my dad as being a shrewd businessman, one who fiercely protected his designs and aggressively went after anyone who infringed on his styles."

She softened her voice and looked up at him with pain-filled eyes. "I have a few images in here" — she pointed to her temple—"of Dad slamming his fist down on a table. His face red with anger."

"I don't know much about the fashion industry, baby, but I understand it's highly competitive and corporate espionage is a common occurrence. To be such a success, your father would have had to be diligent. I don't know a single person who at one time or another hasn't lost their temper. He didn't hit you or your mother. He hit a table, babe. Don't read more into it than is really there. You obviously have his talent and your mother's beauty." He was a little worried she'd decide to take her rightful place as the head of Desman's Designs. There was no doubt in his mind that she was his soulmate and his place was by her side, but he hoped she decided to return to Arizona. He'd never aspired to live in a bustling city.

"Danny was wholly without compassion. He was in pursuit of money, nothing else mattered." She grew contemplative. "Competitors described my dad that same way. What if Dad passed on more than his fashion sense? Something that could be twisted?"

"Alexa, there was never a hint that your father was anything other than a brilliant designer and businessman. And you, my sweet, don't have a cruel bone in your body." He kissed her temple. "Whatever you're thinking, just stop. You're connecting A to B and coming up with D. Just rest, baby. We'll look at all this tomorrow when we've had some much-needed sleep."

"I want to go and see Mr. Hawkings. He worked closely with my parents." Alexa sounded lost in thought.

"We'll go in the morning. Now, let me hold you. I feel like a part of me is missing if you're too far away."

Chapter Sixteen

Alexa was nervous as she stared up at the building she'd been to so often as a child. Mr. Hawkings hadn't been just a business associate, he'd been a friend to her parents. She couldn't remember a single birthday party or celebration without him there. No doubt, he'd have the answers she sought. She just wasn't sure she was strong enough to hear them.

Sid stood by her side, one hand around her waist, and watched her closely. She wished she had something positive to give him, but she felt empty. With Danny gone, all of her ties to the past were completely severed.

"Alexa, it's going to be okay," Sid assured her.

"How can you be so sure, when I'm not?" She wanted to believe him. She wanted it so much she toyed with the idea of getting on a plane and heading back to Arizona before her worst fears could be confirmed.

"Baby, you're always thinking of others. When I found you in the motel room you'd been through hell, but you still asked about Crissy and made sure the other girls were safe. That's not the thought process of a psychopath."

She didn't remember checking on the other victims. She'd been in such pain she'd found it hard to concentrate.

"Mr. Hawkings is waiting on us, baby. He's anxious to see you again. Are you ready to go up?"

Sid looked down at her with such compassion it almost hurt. He thought she was brave and often told her how proud he was of her. She couldn't disappoint him by turning tail and running.

She forced a smile and nodded.

As they entered the lobby, she breathed a sigh of relief and experienced a pang of disappointment at the same time. Everything had changed. The mauve walls and carpet had been replaced with hardwood floors and earth tones. In the elevator, Sid held her tight as they rode to the top floor.

"You can do this, baby."

When the doors opened, she felt like she had entered a time warp. The furnishings had changed, but the view from the glass walls remained virtually the same. She looked to her left, half expecting to see Ms. Gladwin seated behind the elegant cherry desk. Alexa had spent many afternoons sitting on the floor staring out at the buildings. While her dad and Mr. Hawkings had discussed business, she and Ms. Gladwin had passed the time people-watching.

"Ms. Desman, Mr. Hawkings is expecting you. Please go right in." The young woman who greeted them looked nothing like the receptionist Alexa remembered.

As they walked toward the double doors at the far end of the lobby, Alexa looked up at Sid. It had been years since she'd gone by her legal name. She wondered how long it would be before it felt natural.

His gentle smile gave her the encouragement she needed to keep moving.

Sid placed his hand on the small of her back and led her toward the doors. His touch warmed her.

What if her fears were true? What if there was something twisted hiding in her genes? Did she have the strength to walk away from Sid? Could she leave him rather than risk hurting him?

At the entrance, Sid stepped in front of her. She was sure he was using his body to shield her in case of danger. He was constantly thinking of her. When she was with him she felt worthy of love. It was a foreign concept, one she'd been afraid to accept, yet she didn't doubt his sincerity.

After a moment, Sid moved slightly to the right, giving Alexa a clearer view of the office. The first thing she noticed was a framed picture of her parents sitting on a shelf of the bookcase. They looked to be in their mid-twenties. Her dad was gazing at her mom as if she were the moon and stars all rolled into one. It was obvious they were deeply in love.

A sob caught in her throat. She's seen that look before, but she hadn't recognized it for what it was. It was the same look Sid gave to her.

Movement drew her attention. A frail, white-haired gentleman in a wheelchair rolled toward her. Had they passed on the street, she wouldn't have recognized the man before her as the vital, dynamic man she remembered from her youth.

"I don't believe it." He stopped about a foot away and stared up at her.

For some reason, it felt rude to look down at the man her father had respected more than any other. She squatted down and looked for any resemblance of the man she once knew.

"Lexi, I never thought I'd live long enough to see you again. You're the spitting image of your mother." Tears clouded his eyes as he reached out to her.

She grasped his hands and felt him shaking.

Sid's arm moved around her shoulder in support. "Sir, perhaps we could speak more comfortably on the couch."

"Yes, yes, of course. Please excuse my manners." Ethan Hawkings kept a firm grip on Alexa's hand as he worked the controls to maneuver his chair toward the seating area.

Alexa sat near the arm of the sofa so they could maintain contact. "How are you?" she asked, searching his face for clues to his health.

He waved off her concerns. "I tried so hard to find you, Lexi. I hired one private investigator after another. Several times they thought they were getting close, only to have the trail suddenly go cold. But I knew you were alive. I just knew it." His voice shook with conviction.

"I'm so sorry, Mr. Hawkings. Every time I suspected someone was on to me, I'd run. I figured they were Danny's men. I had no idea you were looking for me." Her heart was breaking over eluding his PI's and thus keeping him concerned all those years. "That night, a policeman was outside the studio. When I went to him for help he tried to take me to a warehouse owned by one of Danny's friends. After that, I didn't know who I could trust." She wanted Mr. Hawkings to understand that she hadn't singled him out.

"Danny." He sadly shook his head. "I tried to get him help, but he refused." After a heavy sigh, he continued, "I had suspicions. Nothing concrete, mind you, but enough to know I had to do something. When I filed the papers to have him removed as a signee for the company" — he looked down at his legs — "I was struck by a hit and run driver right outside this office."

"Oh, my God."

"Don't worry yourself, my dear. I get along just fine." He leaned forward and patted her hand. "At the time, I was more angry than anything else. I refused to back down. While I'd been in the hospital, I'd missed my appearance date and had to refile. After he was served again, my house was broken into and my wife's dog was killed. They wrote on the wall in its blood *Bridget's next*." He bowed his head. "I couldn't risk endangering my wife."

"Oh, Mr. Hawkings, I'm so sorry."

"No dear, I'm the one who's sorry. I owed it to your parents to protect you and to get Danny the help he needed. I failed at both."

"You didn't do anything wrong, Mr. Hawkings. No one blames you." She didn't want him feeling guilty on her account. "Do you have any idea what would cause Danny to do these things?"

"Sir, Alexa saw a very ugly side of her brother. It would be very helpful if you could recount your memories of him as a child," Sid interjected.

Mr. Hawkings leaned back in his chair. "It wasn't his fault, Lexi. I've ordered an autopsy to confirm what your parents and I have suspected all along. You were so young you probably don't remember, but as a teen Danny idolized your father and Daniel was shaping him to take over. He was learning every aspect of the business. Each summer, he'd intern in a different department. When he turned sixteen, he went to work in the supply department. They had him driving delivery trucks." A smile touched his lips for the first time. "He absolutely loved it."

"I don't remember any of that." Alexa leaned forward and listened intently.

"You were in Europe with your mom, the south of France I believe. Anyway, Danny was crossing a railroad track when the truck stalled. He panicked. Instead of running, which by all accounts he'd had plenty of time to do, he stayed with the shipment and tried in vain to get the engine started. The locomotive clipped the rear of the truck. It went spinning down a ravine and flipped several times."

When he fell silent Alexa moved to comfort him, but Sid placed a hand on her knee, stopping her.

"Danny broke several bones and I suspect he suffered an undiagnosed head injury. I *know* he became addicted to pain pills." He sounded as if he were lost in a flood of memories. "Daniel and Cheryl didn't want to see it."

Alexa vaguely remembered her parents fighting about Danny, but she'd always gone to her room and worked on her designs rather than pay attention.

"Danny stopped working for the company. He became very withdrawn and surly. On his eighteenth birthday, he was given a twenty-five percent share of Desman's Designs. Your parents had hoped it would re-energize his interest and give him the motivation he needed to apply himself at college."

"It didn't work." She knew he'd washed out of school.

"No. Just the opposite. He got a loan against his shares and bought drugs or gambled it away. I don't know which." He rubbed his index finger along his chin. "As soon as I realized what had happened, I convinced your parents to take measures to protect the business. They got him into a rehab treatment program. We had hoped he'd turn his life around."

"The Desmans died before the business was fully protected." Sid kept the story moving.

Alexa appreciated that Sid jumped over the gory details. She wasn't ready to learn the specifics.

Mr. Hawkings tipped his head and shrugged. "Yes and no. I was able to do a bit of damage control after the fact."

She looked at Sid and he grinned. The same thoughts must have run through both their heads. She didn't want Mr. Hawkings to admit to any wrongdoing so she quickly changed directions. He'd already alleviated her greatest concern. There was no need to relive such painful memories. "Where do we stand with the business? I'd hate to see one of Danny's associates end up with it."

Mr. Hawkings shook his head. "No way. Not as long as I'm alive. On paper, I had controlling interests. Seventy-five percent to be exact. Your parents had set up a trust giving you twenty-five percent of the company on your eighteenth birthday, same as they'd given Danny. The remaining fifty percent was to go to you when you turned twenty-five. Since you didn't come forward and I fought Danny every time he tried to have your status legally changed, it remained under my control."

Status? What a polite way to say have her declared dead.

"Since Danny died without a will and you're his only living blood relative, the company is solely in your possession. It's not nearly as prosperous as it once was, but its net worth is a little over half a billion."

"What?" She couldn't possibly have heard him correctly.

"I'm sorry, Lexi. I did what I could." His shoulders hunched as if he expected to be rebuked.

"Mr. Hawkings," Sid began.

"Please, both of you, call me Ethan," he requested.

Sid glanced at Alexa then started again. "Ethan, Alexa was under the impression that Danny had virtually destroyed the business and it was in need of money."

"Sid's right. How did you manage to keep it going? I just assumed Danny had pillaged the company for everything he could." Her head was swirling. She didn't want to be responsible for her parents' legacy.

"Believe me, he tried." Ethan sat up a little straighter. "I may have misled him concerning the trust fund's fine print. I knew, given the opportunity, he'd run it into the ground. Since I didn't have the expertise or the time to manage the fashion end of it, I sought the help of others. Your dad had teamed with a few of the more renowned academies to offer students an opportunity to showcase their work. I put together a consortium of instructors and fashion world experts to mentor the brightest and most promising young design students as well as those interested in behind the scenes operations to handle the daily minutia. For the most part, they've done an amazing job."

Alexa struggled to process everything Mr. Hawkings was saying and what it meant. "I remember that." She looked at Sid in excitement as memories came rushing back to her. "I can't believe you were able to fulfill my parents' vision. Dad had given a sizable gift to the local university and we'd had a family meeting about it. They had wanted to name the college of arts program after him and he refused. He didn't want to take credit for something that every worker in the company had played a hand in." How could she have doubted her father's character?

She stood and went to Mr. Hawkings. Although she'd follow his request to be called Ethan, he would always be Mr. Hawkings in her mind. Careful to keep her cast from hurting him, she gave him a heartfelt hug. "In my eyes, you're a miracle worker."

"I'm just glad there's something left to give to you. It should have been yours all along. I'm so sorry I failed you, Lexi. You and Danny both. I was never able to get him the help he needed. I'm convinced when the autopsy is completed they're going to find an injury, tumor or something. He was always the sweetest boy." He tipped his head as if considering another possibility. "I suppose it could have just been the drugs, but I'm convinced there's a medical issue that went undiagnosed."

The ultimate cause no longer mattered, at least not to the same extent. Nothing could change the past, but Mr. Hawkings had succeeded in bringing her family's memories alive for her. She'd pushed them so far back into the dark crevices of her mind she'd forgotten what it had meant to be a Desman. Her parents had raised her with a sense of community. They had taught her how important it was to give back, to help others who weren't fortunate enough to have a famous name that opened doors for them.

"Ethan..." It sounded so unnatural to use his first name. "You did everything you could for Danny. By the time anyone suspected anything, he was an adult and you couldn't force him to seek medical treatment. I'm in awe of what you've accomplished. I think it's exactly what my parents would have wanted."

Sid raised her hand to his lips and brushed a kiss in the center of her palm. She leaned into him, grateful he was at her side.

"Your parents would have wanted you and Danny to run the company. I'm convinced the Danny we knew and loved died all those years ago in the truck accident.

But you're here now and the family business will once again have a Desman at the helm."

She didn't want to seem ungrateful, but she'd never aspired to run the company. As a young girl all she'd wanted was to design clothes. Now that she was an adult, she wasn't even sure she wanted to do that on a regular basis, and she knew she didn't want to live in New York. The city terrified her.

Alexa looked up at him with desperation in her eyes. He hoped he wasn't barging in where she didn't want him. "Alexa has forged a life for herself outside of the fashion world. She's built a successful business of her own. It's on a much smaller scale of course. Being on the run, she's had to be careful not to garner too much attention. Yet she managed to make quite the name for herself. She's continued her parents' example of helping others too. She's a major benefactor to numerous women's shelters and animal rescues."

Ethan's eyebrow quirked as if he were suddenly seeing Sid for the first time. "I'm not surprised. In fact, I had the PI's look closely at women working in zoos and veterinary services. Lexi had been instrumental in helping the animals affected during nine-eleven. Tell me about your life, Lexi, and this gentleman you brought with you today." He leaned back into his chair and seemed to study Sid.

Sid felt a wry amusement brewing. It seemed Mr. Hawkings planned to take over the 'protector' role.

Alexa reached over and took his hand. "I don't think I properly introduced you the most important part of my life, Sid Townsend. Without him, I wouldn't be here."

"You did that yourself, babe. It was your courage that brought us here today."

"How did you two meet?"

"A friend of mine from the NYPD had been assigned to investigate Esmerelda's murder. Once the trail grew cold, he turned it over to me. I was working for the FBI at the time. He'd hoped I could find something he'd possibly missed. I chased down countless leads, but came up empty-handed until early this summer." Sid didn't know why he was rambling. Maybe because he couldn't put into words how he'd immediately felt drawn to Alexa.

"One of Danny's men broke into my interior design studio. My secretary called the police. As part of the investigation, they took fingerprints and it was a possible match for a partial print they found on Ezzy. Sid lived in the area and decided to check it out." Alexa's voice grew thick.

"It's all right, baby." He drew her under his shoulder and kissed her temple.

"So many elements of this case just didn't add up that I was never able to let it drop," Sid explained.

Alexa sent him a sexy smirk. "He went undercover to bust a murderess, but ended up with a fiancée instead."

"You're engaged?" Ethan asked in astonishment.

"I haven't managed to scare him off yet," Alexa joked.

"Since you are better aware of Alexa's financial accounts than anyone else, would it be possible for you to write up a prenuptial contract? I'm a lowly federal agent. I don't have any interest in the fashion industry." Sid hoped to alleviate at least a few of the man's concerns.

"Sid, that's not necessary. If I believed for one minute you were after money, I wouldn't marry you," she huffed.

She met his gaze and he could see a storm brewing in her eyes.

"What are your plans, Mr. Townsend?" Ethan asked with his fingers steepled under his chin.

"If I'm to call you Ethan, then I'd appreciate you using my given name as well." Sid knew the man was only making a point, but for Alexa's benefit the conversation needed to stay casual. "I will support Alexa in whatever endeavors she chooses to pursue, but I'm a law enforcement agent and that isn't going to change."

"How do you feel about that, Lexi? Being married to a police officer isn't easy. Their divorce rates are through the roof."

Sid had to give Ethan credit, he had a great poker face. He sounded gruff and displeased, but Sid suspected it was more bluster than anything else. Or maybe that was just wishful thinking.

"He has a talent for finding patterns that others miss. With his gift, he's able to help in a way no one else can. I could never ask him to give that up. While I won't enjoy knowing he's in constant danger, I've learned there are no promises in this life. I'm going to take every minute we have together and live them to the fullest," Alexa answered him somberly.

Sid wished he was wearing a wire so he could hit rewind and hear her last sentence again and again. He hadn't wanted to admit it, even to himself, but he'd been worried that she'd want him to find a niche somewhere in the fashion world. If she'd needed that of him, he would have made the best of it. He'd do just about anything to make her happy. Knowing that she felt the same way about him only proved they were soulmates.

"You aren't moving back to New York, are you?" Ethan asked.

Alexa shook her head. "We're buying some land and starting a horse rescue. I'll take over whatever administrative duties that you need me to for Desman's Designs, but I don't want to change the direction. I think you've captured my parents' vision. I'll facilitate it in any way possible."

"I'll arrange a meeting with the consortium. They'll be relieved to know you're supportive of the status quo." He stared at Alexa for a moment. "I will admit that I'm disappointed I won't be a larger part of your life. I've missed you, Lexi."

Tears filled Alexa's eyes.

"Have you considered retiring to Arizona? The sun shines about three hundred days a year." Sid had already had his fill of cloudy skies. He could imagine Ethan might be ready for a change of scenery.

"After serving on the equestrian board for the last twenty years, I do know a thing or two about horses." Ethan seemed to ponder the idea. "I suppose there are enough shopping centers in the Wild West to keep my wife happy."

Epilogue

Alexa looked up at the star-filled sky as she and Sid walked hand in hand along the candlelit path. Their wedding reception was still in full swing. Both music and laughter echoed off the canyon walls as their friends continued to celebrate.

After being alone for so long, with no true friends to share her life, the sound brought tears to her eyes.

"Are you upset that I didn't want to go to a hotel tonight?" She'd never thought she'd have a real home, somewhere she could put down roots. She couldn't think of a place she'd rather spend their first evening together as husband and wife.

He slid his hand to her ass and gave her teasing swat. "Hell no. For what I have planned, our secluded ranch is much better. I wouldn't want my brothers in blue to show up unannounced."

Alexa bumped her hip into his playfully as she laughed. "Yeah, that might be embarrassing." Considering how vocal she'd become, it was also a real possibility.

As they topped the rise, their house came into view. It was more ostentatious than anything she'd ever expected to own, but she loved every inch of it. It was open, with cathedral ceilings and large, expansive windows. The kitchen was a chef's dream that she was just learning how to use. Aside from the master suite, there were four additional bedrooms. She rubbed her hand protectively over her tummy. If everything continued to go well, in about seven months one of those rooms would have an occupant. One more unexpected gift Sid had given her.

"I love you, Sid."

On the porch, he pulled her into his arms. "And I love you, Alexa. You are my life."

She wrapped her arms around his shoulders as he carried her over the threshold. Alexa didn't care that she was looking at him with stars in her eyes. She loved him and she never wanted him to doubt it.

Sid leaned down and brushed his lips over hers. Sparks crackled between them. She rested her head against his chest as his kiss deepened. His tongue danced with hers, building a fire she knew would never go out. For the first time in her adult life, she'd found a home.

As their lips parted, he allowed her feet to touch the floor. He held her a moment longer, his gaze heated and dominant.

"Go to our room and present for me."

"Yes, Sir." Alexa kissed his cheek demurely. She'd been teasing him all day and she knew he would make her pay for it. Her heart tripped expectantly as she lifted her dress and took off down the hall giggling.

She kicked her shoes in the direction of their large walk-in closet and slid the side zipper down, allowing her to step out of the dress she'd designed for both elegance and easy removal. Their playtime was far beyond anything Alexa had ever considered possible. She didn't want anything as inconsequential as a dress to get in the way.

On the bed, she noticed Sid had laid out several bundles of their new teal hemp ropes next to a towel. Considering how bumpy it was, she knew it hid several toys. She was tempted to peek, but she decided the thrill of surprise was better.

Alexa took a deep breath then dropped to her knees on a pad next to Sid's side of the bed. She criss-crossed her hands and linked her fingers behind her back and waited. Her excitement was palpable. It took a few moments to clear her head.

Sid stopped in the doorway with his tie and shirt in his hand. "I am a lucky, lucky man." He tossed his clothes on top of her dress. "I want to see you, just like that, every evening. Will you do that for me?"

She couldn't keep the smile from touching her lips. "With pleasure." The look on his face and the bulge in his pants was something she wanted to see again and again.

"Are you ready, baby?"

"I was born ready." She infused amusement into her voice, but it was the truth. She believed she was meant to be with Sid.

Sid chuckled then bent down and picked her up. He tossed her on the bed. "Lay on your stomach with your hands behind your back."

Sid wrapped two strands of rope around her wrists. The tails danced across her thigh and along her ass cheek as he made three passes. Her breath caught in her chest when he tightened the knot.

"How does that feel, Mrs. Townsend?" he whispered near her ear.

"Strict," she answered, anxious for more.

"I'm just getting started." He grabbed another bundle and began securing her ankles. "You made Ethan a very happy man this afternoon."

"It was sweet of him to give me away. I'm so glad he and Bridget decided to move near us." She was finding it hard to concentrate as the fibers vibrated with each pass Sid made.

"He sure knows his way around a horse. It's embarrassing that an old man can ride circles around me, but I am picking up a few pointers from him," Sid grumbled.

Alexa laughed. "I'm sure you could show him a thing or two about knots."

"Damn straight." He swatted her ass. "Spread your legs."

"How?" she complained. "You tied my feet together."

"Bend your knees," he ordered as he pulled her feet closer to her butt. "I'm so glad your wrist is healed. I've been thinking about this position for a while now. I love how much control it gives me."

"As if that matters. You may torture me for a bit, but you always bring me great pleasure." So much so that she craved their alone time together. Each scene he planned felt more intense than the last. It was frightening and exhilarating at the same time.

"Remember that as you beg me to stop."

Her stomach bottomed out and her pussy grew wetter. Would he push her that far again? God, she hoped so.

Sid pulled another section of hemp from the pile he'd laid on the bed. The bindings at her ankles tightened seconds before she felt more vibrations along her wrists.

Her heart fluttered as he drew her into a taut bow. The muscles along her back strained to comply. Her brain slowed as she forced her body to relax and remain pliant.

"Good girl. I love the way you give yourself into my keeping." Sid pulled her hair into a ponytail and secured it with a thin piece of rope.

She felt something brush along each shoulder and she realized he was braiding the rope into her hair. Her mind whirled for a moment as she considered what he must have planned. She didn't have long to ponder. Alexa groaned as he attached the rope to the bindings at her ankles. The discomfort bordered on painful as she tested to see how much movement was available to her. To ease the ache at her scalp, she had to arch her back at a wholly unnatural angle.

"You've been a brat all day. Are you ready to face the consequences?"

"Yes." She smiled. Throughout the day she'd teased him, knowing he wouldn't have the opportunity to do anything about it.

Sid grasped her arms and moved her around until her breasts were resting off the edge of the bed.

"I suggest you keep your wiggling to a minimum." He chuckled, as if finding her precarious position amusing.

She knew he would never let her fall, but the sheer possibility heightened her need.

Alexa's pussy clenched as Sid kicked off his shoes and unzipped his tuxedo pants, allowing his cock to spring free. She licked her lips in anticipation.

"This morning at breakfast, you were incorrigible. I warned you I would exact my revenge and you just laughed. You obviously need a lesson in respect."

She couldn't help but smile remembering his discomfort as she'd reached under the table and begun stroking his cock. Ethan and Bridget had been seated in the bench across from them.

"You were merciless as you brought me to the brink time and time again.

"I'm sorry." She giggled. "You handled it very well, though. I'm sure our guests had no idea."

He gave the cheek of her ass a loud smack. "Like hell you're sorry."

"It was fun," she admitted.

"You're going to learn payback's a bitch, baby. I'm going to torture you until I come. I suggest you use that highly talented mouth of yours to the best of your ability." He laughed as if he knew something she didn't.

Alexa was eager to begin. Sucking his cock always made her needy as hell, and the strict position he'd tied her in already had her wanting to play.

"Open wide, brat."

With her ponytail attached to her ankles she didn't really have any choice in the matter and they both knew it. He used her shoulders to rock her forward and back as he fucked her mouth. After a few strokes, he paused and withdrew.

"Feels good, doesn't it, baby?" He gazed down at her with love.

"Yes, it does." Something in his tone told her he was toying with her. She knew she was in trouble. A naughty thrill coursed through her, pebbling her nipples.

"But you need more don't you?"

More? "Well, I think you do. I had just barely gotten started."

He grabbed the rope securing her hands to her feet and steadied her as he walked around to the other side of the bed. She couldn't see what he was doing, but she remembered the items he'd hidden under the towel.

"This should make the game a little more interesting," he mused, before flipping the switch to their Hitachi.

"Oh God." She was already aroused and knew she wouldn't last long. Would he turn it off once she came? She knew the odds weren't in her favor. Alexa attempted to bow her head in defeat, but the rope held her firmly in his control.

Being completely at his mercy had her teetering on the edge. Fear mingled with desire as he strapped the vibrator to her thigh using his discarded belt.

"How are you doing, baby?" He rubbed his thumb along her cheek.

Forming words was beyond her ability, but she nodded as much as the ropes would allow her.

"If you need to stop wiggle your fingers. That will be your safeword for the time being. Show me that you understand."

She frantically moved her hands, needing him to give her access to his cock again. There was no way she could hold out for long, though she was learning she could somewhat modulate the intensity along her clit by moving her leg farther to the side. The problem was it pulled like the dickens at her ankles and scalp.

"Hungry, baby?" he asked devilishly.

"Yes," she whispered before opening her mouth wider.

She groaned as his hard cock slid between her lips. With her tongue, she swirled around the ridge as he began to rock her back and forth. On the outward stroke she screamed as the vibrator pressed firmly against her clit, sending her into a strong orgasm. Her eyes felt as if they'd rolled back in her head as he fucked her mouth. After a few moments the thrums of pleasure slowed enough that she could catch her breath and she heard him murmuring to her.

"That was beautiful, baby. So pretty. I can't wait to watch your next one."

She tried to shake her head, but each turn yanked her hair fiercely. The Hitachi continued to buzz. To ease the torture on her clit, she was forced to keep the ropes pulled taut.

"Time to take it to the next level."

What? Before her brain could engage enough to form the word, her gaze fell to the butt plug Sid was holding out for her to see.

"You always come so much harder when your kegel has something to clamp on to."

The magnitude of the situation she was in finally became clear.

He took his time applying the lube to the glistening stainless steel shaft. As his fingers slid the length of it and twisted along the neck, she knew she was lost. By the time *he* came, there'd be nothing left of her.

Sid coated the entrance of her ass and pushed the plug against her opening. Just as he'd taught her, she pushed back, allowing it to fill her. Before she knew it, the toy was in place, and just that fast the pleasure started to build again.

She licked her lips, silently begging him to give her his cock.

"Eager, aren't you, my love?"

As he plundered her mouth, she noticed he was absolutely rock-hard. She tried to ignore the demonic device sending her clit into a nuclear meltdown and focus on bringing Sid as much pleasure as he always gave her, but it was damn near impossible. Each time she moved, the wand made direct contact. She fought the sensations as best she could. Sweat beaded on her forehead as she concentrated, but it was too much.

Her second orgasm tore through her with more force than the first. She trembled with each aftershock.

"You almost got me on that one. God, you're breathtaking." Sid kissed her forehead and ran his hands down her arms and squeezed her feet.

While his touch was pure heaven, she knew he wasn't finished with her. He'd promised to torture her until she safeworded or he came, and she'd learned over the last few months that Sid always kept his word.

Desperation was a living, breathing entity residing inside her now. She didn't know how much more she could take, but she'd be damned if she was going to safeword on their wedding night.

Sid grasped her breast and pinched her nipple until she moaned. "Oh, I'm sorry, baby. Please forgive me for being so neglectful. The girls want attention too, don't they?"

She heard the jangling of clamps and knew what he had in store for her. As the metal bit into the tender peak, sending fire through the left side of her chest, her brain rebelled. "No, don't do it. I can't take any more."

A rumble of laughter shook his chest as he clamped her other nipple. "Don't be silly, baby. You'd be angry with me if I left you lopsided."

He knew her so well. Had he stopped, she really would have been disappointed. She also had complete faith that if she wiggled her fingers, he'd not only stop, but have her out of the bindings so fast it would make her head spin.

"Are you ready to come for me one more time, Mrs. Townsend?"

Her body was thrumming as her third orgasm started to build. She managed to form the words, "Bring it," as she sent him a playful wink.

He growled as he thrust his cock into her mouth. Each stroke took him deep. The chain on the clamps bounced against the mattress, accentuating the erotic bite along her tender nipples.

His balls grew tight, telling her he was close. Sweet victory was within reach. She relaxed her throat muscles and took him deeper. On the outward stroke, she swirled her tongue over the head, reveling in feel of him. He slid home as the initial surge from her third orgasm began. Sid's guttural shout signaled he was right there with her. Together they rode each wave of pleasure.

"Oh, baby, one of these days you're gonna kill me doing that." Sid sat tailor fashion on the ground beside the bed as if his legs could no longer hold him up. "Hang on, this is going to smart a bit," he warned her as he unclipped the first nipple clamp.

She whimpered and struggled against the bindings until Sid's mouth eased the ache. His touch turned the discomfort into sweet delight. He removed the other clamp before she could worry too much about it. Immediately, he swirled his tongue over the nipple.

After a few moments, he stood and began removing the restraints. "One day soon, I'm going to take pictures of you bound like this. I want you to see how erotic the ropes look against your skin."

"I'd like that." They'd spent a lot of time talking about the traumatic experiences she'd gone through. They both knew they weren't going to just disappear, but Sid had been patiently replacing each terrifying memory with new ones. When he grabbed her from behind, instead of reliving the rape, she now anticipated his fingers tickling her until she laughed so hard tears rushed down her cheeks. The smell of smoke reminded her of their evenings making love in front of their outdoor firepit. Sid had earned her trust. She believed he'd never hurt her, and if she needed more time he'd always give it.

"Scoot to the middle of the bed, Alexa. I'm going to draw a bath." Sid waited until she was safely in the center of the mattress.

Shortly after the water had begun to fill the tub, Alexa smelled her favorite bath salts. She closed her eyes as the eucalyptus and spearmint scent brought a flood of soothing memories.

"No napping allowed, Mrs. Townsend. We've only just begun."

About the Author

Tori lives in the beautiful Sonoran Desert with her loving husband of almost thirty years. She wakes up each morning to the howls of coyotes and the barking of her family dogs wanting to join the fray.

When Tori isn't writing, she's either spending time with her two, wonderful adult children, or creating stained glass art.

She likes her love stories scorching hot. She tries to infuse a fire and passion between her characters that rivals the blazing summer sun that Arizona is known for. Tori encourages you to bask in the heat between the covers of a Dominant/submissive, happily-ever-after, bondage romance.

Tori Carson loves to hear from readers. You can find her contact information, website and author biography at http://www.totallybound.com.

TOTALLY
BOUND

Home of Erotic Romance

www.ingramcontent.com/pod-product-compliance
Lightning Source LLC
Chambersburg PA
CBHW030129180626
46812CB00002B/620